DATE DUE

SEP 23 1993		

GAYLORD No. 2333   PRINTED IN U.S.A.

SLAKE'S LIMBO

SLAKE'S LIMBO

BY FELICE HOLMAN

CHARLES SCRIBNER'S SONS • New York

Charles Scribner's Sons
Macmillan Publishing Company
866 Third Avenue, New York, NY 10022
Collier Macmillan Canada, Inc.

Printed in the United States of America

First Edition

11 13 15 17 19———20 18 16 14 12 10

Library of Congress Catalog Card Number 74-11675
ISBN 0-684-13926-X

AREMIS SLAKE, at the age of thirteen,
took his fear and misfortune and
hid them underground. The thing is,
he had to go with them.

SLAKE'S LIMBO

The thing that happened, when finally it happened, was so perfectly logical that it should not really be considered surprising. Because the fact is that even earlier in life Aremis Slake had often escaped into the subway when things got rough above ground. He kept a subway token in his pocket for just that emergency, and the emergencies kept occurring due to a joining of hostile circumstances.

To begin with, Slake was small. Anyone could beat him for any reason or non-reason, and did, when they could catch him. But he was wiry and wily, too, and he could often out-run, tack, back-track, double-back, and finally dodge unseen into the subway, hiding, if possible, in some nook of the station to save the fare, or riding, if necessary, till things cooled off and the world above became habitable again. That's just to begin with.

Slake was useless to any gang. This was learned early in his life. Poor vision made him a clumsy thief, and a severe reaction to smoke and drugs made him a bad risk in other ways. On two occasions when he had been conned into taking pills, he had ended up in the hospital. He became a pariah. When not shunned entirely, he was hunted and hounded for sport.

Other than that, Slake dreamed and walked a dreamer. Though usually hungry, he hardly ever

3

dreamed of things to eat. Sometimes he dreamed of being "stronger than" or "bigger than," of looming over and hitting back. But more often he dreamed of "somewhere else"—anywhere else. But where? And dreaming thus led him into lamp posts, up to ankles in puddles, up to elbows in spilled things, sprawling down school stairways, while teachers scolded and classmates scoffed, pushing him down again as soon as he gained his feet.

All this was aggravated by Slake's glasses . . . or lack of them. Regularly broken, they were finally abandoned entirely. Then the world beyond ten feet became a fog through which people came and went, vehicles appeared and disappeared, holes broke open beneath his feet, stairs descended precipitously, and lamp posts loomed and struck. Slake got his lumps.

Well, that is in the past. But for the purpose of this chronicle of events, it is simplest and most practical and even sufficient to believe that Slake was born an orphan at the age of thirteen, small, nearsighted, dreaming, bruised, an outlander in the city of his birth (and in the world), a lad of shifting fitful faith with a token in his pocket. In other ways he was not so different from the rest of the young raised with house keys around their necks, rearing themselves in the litter-strewn streets.

When, after school, Slake dragged up the dark stairway to the apartment where he lived—smelling it, hearing it—he felt it was not more than he deserved since he was, by the testimony of teachers, classmates, and the humans who inhabited the space in which he slept (and sometimes ate), a worthless lump. A worthless lump, he was slapped up in the morning by a kind of aunt. A worthless lump, he stood in front of the wheezing refrigerator, gnawing at what came to hand. He poured cold coffee into his worthless lump of a stomach and took his worthless lump of a body to school, passing on his stairway and in doorways, the lumps of other humans who had come to rest thus.

Later, his cold and empty stomach would remind him of what his nearsighted eyes could barely see on the classroom clock—lunchtime. When the bell declared this true, a variety of scraps, having nothing to do with each other or with any organized meal, would be fished from Slake's pocket and called lunch.

But sometimes, late and without even his coffee, Slake would arrive at school at or after the last bell. He would fall into his seat and receive the teacher's scolding through the blood pounding in his ears. And once (Slake's luck!) he arrived in this condition on a day when it was his turn to hold the flag.

5

"Class stand. Aremis!"

Gasping, coughing, cold in belly, cold in hand and foot, Slake stood in front of the class and held the flag, the muscles behind his knees twitching.

"I pledge allegiance . . . ," more or less in unison, except for Slake. The teacher held up a hand shaking with annoyance.

"Just because you are holding the flag, Mr. Slake, you are not excused from reciting. Begin again."

"I pledge allegiance to the flag . . . the United . . . of . . ." Slake's voice faded. ". . . the Republic for which . . ." and Slake's knees unhinged as he let the flag slip from his fingers and he hit the floor before it did.

In the place he called his home, overlooking the elevated subway tracks, Slake slept on a cot in the kitchen, and there he had a dream so frequent and so familiar that it became as much a part of waking as of sleeping. Just before he awoke, it seemed, Slake would dream that a bird had come to the sooty window, open just enough to keep him from asphyxiating . . . that it had come to the sill and perched there, perilously near the inner edge so that it might, at any moment, fall or fly into the room. In his fear that this small creature of the air might blunder into this hostile place, Slake would open his mouth to cry out. As he did so, the bird would lean forward and land in Slake's mouth. Then Slake swallowed it.

Slake would awake gagging. The first feeling of the bird choking him would give way to the wide-awake feeling of the bird pecking at his ribs. Often, when he awoke, he could hear it cry.

In all this hostile world was there no one for Slake? For some time there was one—Joseph. Because of some situation in his head, Joseph wore a perpetual smile and a perpetually blank look. Joseph did not read, nor even speak much, but around Joseph there was an area of calm and Slake sought him out. They would stand silently together on a corner and Joseph would occasionally give Slake a tap on the back.

Joseph and Slake often took long walks together up and down and around the streets of their neighborhood, past boarded-up buildings, vacant lots full of junk, scrawled walls which announced names, called obscenities. They wandered through crowds, not seeing them. In good weather, people and animals leaned out of windows to watch the life below. On hot days, the hydrants poured water on screaming children and set the garbage afloat. Ambulances and police cars screeched by. Wash hung limply on fire escapes. Old men picked through junk piles.

On a large boulevard about ten blocks from Slake's street, there were some old row houses which had small front yards. These houses had large stoops—almost porches. On one of these was a bench that fascinated Slake and he often walked the distance just to see it. It was made from the headstone of a grave balanced on two footstones.

"Whadya think, Joseph? They steal it off a grave?" Joseph did not answer but Slake did not wait for Joseph to answer questions. "Or maybe the guy in the house has this stone all ready for hisself."

Slake liked that version—the owner sitting on the headstone now to take his ease in the sunny afternoon, and later, lying under it . . . forever.

It had been nice to walk with Joseph.

Why, Slake wondered, did the boys not harass Joseph? The answer could be one that Slake only sensed, but did not really know—that Joseph was mystical—peace in war, happiness in misery, sun in rain.

Over the summer vacation a truck hit Joseph. There was no one for Slake.

So, the day of the sweater—the end of the beginning. Slake had found the sweater on the seat of a subway car only days before. Blue and gray diamond-patterned and nearly new. The day he had worn it to school, they had pulled it off his body, forcing his arms over his head, twirling him around until the sweater pulled

8

free. They had grabbed it, waved it in the air, tossed it high above his head like a football while he ran this way and that trying to get it back.

"Over here, Alfie!"

"Big Joe! Hup, hip!"

"Zeke! Over here!"

"Here y'ar, Slake, man! Here y'ar." A fake offer. Slake moved in for the promise to be kept.

"Hip, hup!" and over his head.

Then, as one, they moved towards him—a pack—the sweater held high now on a broom handle. And then the chase began, around the parking meters and fruit stands, through the alleys and junkyards, and had to end, as always, with more lumps and bruises or, if not, with escape into the subway.

Down in the subway it was, and Slake's dreams of being stronger than, bigger than, or even strong enough, big enough, slipped with his grasp on the handsome, eighty percent reprocessed wool, nearly new sweater. Chased to the last ditch, he paid his token and leaped onto a train, just leaving.

The subway clattered and swayed its way downtown, and Slake with the instinct of other migratory creatures flew from the train at Seventy-seventh Street and Lexington Avenue. This was an unusual move in itself; Slake usually exited only at transfer points. Now he

9

could not get home without the payment of another token, which he did not have.

He came up onto the street in a neighborhood that he had never seen before, walked two blocks uptown to the splendid width of Seventy-ninth Street, and started to walk westward. Here were sparkling shops, large clean buildings, and neatly tended saplings along the edge of the relatively unlittered pavement. The absence of tin cans, garbage, and other refuse, the scarcity of steps and stoops, and the lack of people sitting or leaning about them interested Slake. As he crossed Park Avenue he waited on the curb with respect as a young delivery boy drove a bicycle through heavy traffic as if it were a fine car. He continued along Seventy-ninth and finally crossed Fifth Avenue and walked into the fall landscape of Central Park.

At the sight of the park, something came back to Slake. It was the recurrence of an old fantasy that *this year the leaves would stay on the trees.* Though there were few trees in Slake's life, this thought returned to him year after year. Now he broke into a run, winding and spinning through paths of the park, kicking up a kaleidoscope of fallen leaves, while above some leaves remained tenuously on the branches. Slake ran twenty blocks south, and well into the park. He was far from home . . . far from home, but his failing faith had given way once again to hope . . . a last hope. Slake, without sweater or subway token, put his faith in nature.

"This is the year . . . ," said Slake as he ran, "*this* is the year the leaves *will* stay on the trees." And the enthusiasm of this hope in this new territory, and the momentary strength of this conviction made Slake heady. He looked about quickly and saw only an old lady dozing on a bench. Her mouth was open; her hair looked borrowed. Slake grabbed a bunch of tall dried grass from the foot of a poorly tended maple tree, leaped into its low branches and, squinting against the sun, tied several of the remaining leaves securely to the branches.

That was Slake at the tallest, strongest moment of his life till then. It lasted *just* a moment. Shouts broke into his ambitious dream as a park attendant appeared, running, shouting, and waving a rake.

"Get down out of there, you bum kid!"

Slake blinked.

"Get down, I said!" The attendant poked at the tree with his rake, but Slake had moved out of reach. "The cops, then!" and the man was off and running to a nearby phone. The old lady awoke and started pointing.

Slake, now entirely ripped from his dream, abandoned it on the branch, leaped to the ground, spun around twice, ran several hundred yards through the park and out of it, down a flight of stairs and, committing still another crime, ran frantic and tokenless under the turnstile and into the subway at Columbus Circle.

He stayed one hundred and twenty-one days.

2 Slake rode the subway all that afternoon, crisscrossing the city, cutting it to pieces with the crashing cars, slicing through tunnels, burrowing through rock. He sat, a catapulted mummy, resurrecting himself from time to time, to exit at a transfer point, and enter another train headed to some other distant corner of the metropolitan subway system. It did not matter to Slake which corner. He touched base in the Bronx, Queens, Brooklyn, doubled back and clattered into the Upper West Side. Then, down again to the Battery and back again, finally to exit at the Forty-second Street station of the Lexington Avenue line— Grand Central Station.

What drew Slake from his getaway train at this particular place? Ask what put him on it. Something took him through the maze, the crush of people shoving each other through the turnstiles to a staircase. Slake started up. It was a crucial move.

But as he began to climb the stairs, a flying squadron of boys descended. A phalanx of leaping weight on the hoof, they appeared above him and seemed to fall thumping, jumping, yowling down the stairs faster than inertia and gravity should allow. Reality seized Slake by the throat and released his heels. He turned and ran, the sound of pounding feet mixed with the pounding blood in his ears. Back towards the platform ran

13

Slake, committing the third crime of the day—under the turnstile and down the nearest flight of stairs.

"Stop him!" yelled the man in the change booth to no one who cared. But Slake ran as if pursued, through the station, past the dispatcher's windowed office to the very end of the platform; and realizing that it was, indeed, the end, leaped off without a backward look and ran into the tunnel.

He had run only twenty paces when he awoke from his nightmare to the awareness of where he was and what he was doing—feet in a track bed, hands gripping gritty walls—terror behind, blackness ahead. Slake froze where he was, his spine pulling him back against the wall, away from the rails, away from any possible oncoming trains.

Oncoming trains!

Slake reached wildly for what he knew he should find—something he had seen many times from the station and the train itself—concrete alcoves in which the track workmen could stand while the trains were passing. Stepping carefully on the wood covering of the third rail, inching along, his hands groped for an alcove, but before they found one, they found something else—a hole—a jagged opening in the subway wall!

Slake bent forward, and in the dim light that came from the nearby tunnel lights, Slake could make out what looked like walls on the other side of the hole. With shaking and numbed limbs, Slake moved through this opening, slipping a leg through first, feeling for solid ground and finding it, and then snaking the rest of his body through. He stood up carefully, not sure of the height of his rabbit hole. He hit nothing, and his feet were not on track bed but on flat rock and a few loose stones and timbers.

Slake moved slowly—a blind man who was beginning to see—and found that he was in a small enclosure whose only opening was the jagged entrance, left by fallen concrete, through which he had just come. Unoccupied and unused, it appeared to be, for want of a better term, a "room" in the subway. Slake sat down with his back against the farthest wall. Indeed, as it ultimately turned out, *Slake moved in.*

The excellence of Slake's hideout—Slake's new home—was a result of (1) misjudgment; (2) a hot summer's day; (3) the evil influences of alcohol, and other fortuitous circumstances which Slake did not know and would never know. But, nevertheless, it may just as well be told that Slake's room no longer had anything to do with the subway. It really had more to do with the Commodore Hotel, against whose wall he now leaned.

When the Commodore Hotel was being built,

15

things were not so different in some ways than they are now; things went wrong. They went wrong on a lucky day years and years before Slake was born. On that very hot day, in the second decade of the century, two workmen named Coggins and Murone were blasting in the depths of the hotel's excavations. Recovering as they were from a cooling liquid lunch, they lost count and set too big a charge of dynamite, and at the wrong angle at that. This extended the foundations of the Commodore an unexpected distance, breaking through the wall of rock that would have divided the hotel from the subway. This exposed and enlarged one of the many small "caves" made during the construction of the subway for the temporary storage of equipment. As the subway work progressed, the caves were covered over by the advancing tunnel walls.

Having broken through to this one, Coggins and Murone were properly humbled by the foreman and were set to shoring up the wall to offset any possible loss of lateral support. They erected some steel framing and covered the Manhattan schist with reinforced concrete. All secure, they closed the side connecting it to the Commodore Hotel, leaving behind a small room with no doors or windows.

Over the years that followed, the concrete wall of the subway tunnel suffered the wear and tear of time, temperature, and vibration. Hairline

16

cracks formed and spread, causing bits of concrete to crumble and fall, finally opening up Slake's room, prepared for him through the courtesy of Mr. Coggins and Mr. Murone of the Commodore's construction crew more than half a century before he needed it.

What this leads to is the inescapable truth that Aremis Slake—worthless lump, optimist of the leaves, renegade, and toll-jumper—now took his ease in a room that was not in the jurisdiction of the IRT subway, but was, in fact, a structural part of the Commodore Hotel.

It is hard to say what changes this could have made in Slake if this cheerful fact were known to him. But since it is only one of the many unknown cheerful facts that operated to affect or not affect him, it is fairly safe to say that the simple practical result—the existence of the room and his presence in it—were all that really mattered.

ON ANOTHER TRACK

As Slake rested and then slept, many trains came to a stop at the station and then pulled out and passed Slake's cave. One of these trains was driven by a motorman named Willis Joe Whinny.

Willis Joe had not started out to be a motorman. When he was very young, what he had aimed to do was to work on a sheep station in Australia. It was a very strong wish which had started on a rainy Saturday afternoon, in this way: What Willis Joe liked to do best on Saturdays was to go down to Randall's Island, under the Triborough Bridge, and jog around the track. Willis Joe liked to run because it made all thoughts go right out of his mind and the only thing that mattered was that one more lap. But on rainy Saturdays he used to go to the movies with the kids he hung around with.

Right now, if you were to ask him, Willis Joe could not tell you what the feature picture had been at the Loew's Astoria on the particular rainy afternoon that gave him his ambition, but he could tell you in detail what the short feature was. It was a film about sheep ranching on a station in Australia—hundreds of thousands of acres of endless horizon.

Up until then Willis Joe had no idea at all what he wanted to be. But those men who herded the sheep were strong—you should see them throw those big sheep when they sheared them. The men sat on tall horses and had wonderful, faithful dogs who helped herd the sheep. The whole setup appealed strongly to Willis Joe who had never been on a horse, whose horizons were blocked by tall buildings, and whose landlord would not let him have a dog. And he liked the idea of managing all those sheep.

A train passes by. It is driven by a motorman who dreams of driving sheep in Australia. In what way can this have anything to do with Aremis Slake?

3 Slake sat, his back against the wall, his heart a racing machine, his spirit a frightened cat, his limbs a weak and uncoordinated collection of gears. His head dropped. His chin rested on his chest. He did not sleep, but in a state of nearly suspended being, sat without moving for uncounted hours.

Trains taking people to, taking people fro, came braking to a stop at the station, then started up and ground past his cave. They might not have been there at all; they did not cause Slake to blink. But at some point the trains came less frequently. Quiet moments filled the tunnel. It had the effect of stirring Slake. He looked up. He looked around.

Light from the tunnel bulbs reached dimly into his room. He blinked. It was quite possible, now that he was used to it, to see where he was. He was in a room that measured about four feet wide and about eight feet long, with a low ceiling. The walls were of cement with steel beams; the floor was rock with a scattering of loose stones and a few boards. That was all. His bearings established, Slake settled his back against the wall of the Commodore Hotel and breathed a little more easily.

If Slake had had the gift of seeing up and around corners—periscopic vision—he would have seen the front entrance of the Commodore

Hotel on Forty-second Street, old but still handsome. He would have seen taxicabs and automobiles of distinction gently depositing valuable people in front of portals, through which they would pass to walk upon carpets that sank like quicksand. And Slake was part of all this! That he did not know it is merely a comment on consciousness. That is to say, one could be carried out to sea and drowned while asleep, and the fact that one had been unconscious and unaware would not cancel out the fact that one had, indeed, drowned.

So, Slake, on the underside of the stones, several layers down—beneath floors, beneath furnaces, beneath chutes and pipes, beneath cement—was, nevertheless, very much a unit of the Commodore Hotel, not the less a haven, not the less a center of comfort, not the less Slake's foothold in the world only because he did not know it.

On the flip side of the coin, of course, is the fact that the Commodore Hotel had a dimension of which the corporate "it" was also unaware—a secret closet in its nether regions, a chamber for which it received no rent, and now a charity for which it received no thanks . . . nor tax deduction.

What other unknown dimensions could this one suggest!

Now, after the long hours of tension, Slake settled into a kind of rising and falling sleep pattern. In its depths he was dreamless; but as he rose to semi-wakefulness, muddied pictures came to his eyes. Out of his memory Slake reconstructed a past. Where had it been? The more recent and intolerable present had blurred it, dulled it. Yet now his early childhood, which had been so short he scarcely ever recalled it, returned. He saw himself—Aremis—in some rural place where he had been sent as a fresh-air child to breathe someone else's fresh air.

In the enormous backyard of the house. . . . Whose house? In the backyard there was a small, perfect model farmyard, and in a pen was a clean, clean pig. And the children of the house used to swing on the clean white gate of the clean pen for fun and sport. While the pig nibbled its constant meal, the children would fling the gate open and ride the gate back to its closed position. And while the gate was open, the pig would turn and run towards it, but before the pig could get there the children, screaming, would swing the gate closed just in time. "In the knick of time," they'd say. In the knick of time, except once. It was the once that Slake was now remembering.

The gate had swung open and the pig had run towards it, but somehow the children's timing was off. The gate stayed open too long. Out and running came the pig, and the children, laughing first but then screaming with mock terror and delight, were running in front of it. And Slake was running too, but he was not laughing and if any sound came from his mouth it would not have been mock anything. Now out of the house came the mother and father and two nuns in their habits. Slake thought he was running for his life down the street behind the other two children, and behind him (too close) the pig, and behind the pig the father of the children, and behind him two nuns running in a black and white cloud. Slake running and running. Home? Where?

In his cave, Slake had stopped running for a time, and he slept.

4 In the early hours of the next day it occurred to Slake that he was not being sought by the police, that he was not the main object of a great crime hunt or even part of a general crackdown. The feeling of freedom and release that came to him then was immense. His fast for the last many hours made him dizzy; his cramped position made him unsteady; and both conditions made him weak enough to feel that this revelation had come to him as a vision. A mystical being had entered his cell crying, "Slake, you are free. Arise!" Slake, already arisen, now put his head out of the porthole. Damp but free air came to him in drafts. Dimness and dampness were the primary qualities of this atmosphere of the subway tunnel, but one could also sense other elements. Slake selected something that smelled like gasoline and something that smelled like onions and peanuts. The gasoline didn't interest him, but the peanuts did. Madly.

He put his head out of the porthole and checked the length of the tunnel for oncoming trains. He saw and heard none. Keeping his eye on the great crocodile of the third rail, he eased out of his cave and, holding close to the wall until he was near the mouth of the tunnel, made his way down the track. Then he crossed the track and from below the level of the platform

24

peered up at the dispatcher's office. There was a man in it and Slake was taking no chances. He slid under the overhang of the platform and crept, unseen, down the entire length of the station just under the platform edge. This brought him to the far end of the station. Standing up he could see people waiting for trains down towards the center stairway, quite a distance from him. He sneaked up the few steps used by track workers and tried to look like someone who had just arrived at the station to catch a train. He was very successful. For one of the few times in his life Slake experienced fleeting confidence. "I'm an actor . . . a great actor." But this was an over-statement and Slake knew it.

Slake now climbed a flight of stairs and near the turnstiles he discovered the aroma that he had thought was gasoline. It wasn't. It was an unbelievably strong disinfectant being used in the men's room, and its intensity singed his nostrils and throat. Slake investigated the facility. The human being who had been selected for this work was just departing, leaving a newly washed floor. His work may have been thankless until then, but Slake was thankful. His experience of school, tenement, and subway lavatories was wide enough to afford him the knowledge that this was a rare moment approaching cleanliness and thus godliness. He took advantage of the situation—lavished water all over his face and arms, drank water from his cupped hands, and used the toilet.

As Slake slapped water about extravagantly, he was aware that this may have been one of the few mornings of his life within memory that he had not been otherwise slapped or shouted into wakefulness, dragged from solitary sleep into the crowded and threatening day. Here he stood, dripping cold water, shivering, but feeling vaguely and oddly unhounded. He ran his wet fingers through his hair, drying them thus, and began to consider his empty stomach. He had no idea what the possibilities might be.

Slake went out into the wide area which served as a concourse for people going in all directions. A mass of passengers coming from the uptown local now surged through and Slake allowed himself to be caught up in the pooled momentum. They seemed to be pushing him into an arcade, but nobody paid the least attention to him.

"They don't even notice me," Slake thought. "It's like I'm invisible."

But he could see himself reflected in the dirty glass of the still-closed shops and he knew that he was not invisible, though it was a wish he often had. In fact, it surprised him even more to see that, except that he had no jacket, his reflection looked not too different from everyone else's. This reminded him that he was not only hungry, he was quite chilly. Both of these discomforts were familiar to Slake; they were not devastating conditions. They were accepted to a point, like other harassments and discomforts.

And then Slake was passing a glass window behind which some people were standing at a counter or sitting on stools. They seemed to be eating in the quickest way anyone could eat or drink, somewhat the same way Slake ate, standing before the refrigerator most mornings. Slake stopped to watch, pressing his face against the glass so he could see better. Customers tapped impatient coins waiting to be served, and when the coffee came they tossed the liquid down as though there were no need to swallow. Slake watched through the glass as if he were watching a motion picture. One man, leather briefcase between his ankles, waved his hand at the counter girl who moved without nerves to serve the morning brew. Slowly she drew steaming black coffee from the steel urn and set the mug before the man. He threw down a coin and started to sip the coffee. He frowned, and then sipped again. It was too hot for him. Did he have a more sensitive gullet than the others? He looked at his watch, grabbed his briefcase, and left. Fury was marked in black lines around his eyes and raked upon his forehead. The cup of coffee stood steaming where he had left it. *Slake moved in.*

His heart raced as he put himself in front of the mug. He had never before in his life stood at a counter like this with people dressed for business or whatever. He didn't know what he expected, but it surprised him when it didn't happen. He waited. He reached out and picked up the mug. It was still very hot. Slake noticed people helping themselves to wrapped lumps of sugar from bowls along the counter. He reached out and quickly took a lump. He took another, then watched the cubes absorb the coffee color and essence before they dissolved. Then Slake took a third lump, unwrapped it, and dipped it just a little into the coffee. Then he ate the piece of sugar which had drawn the hot coffee up into itself. It was delicious. Now he sipped the coffee from the mug and the hot sweet drink warmed Slake in the stomach, throat, neck, and everywhere. His heart stopped racing. When he looked up sideways at the counter girl, she did not seem surprised that he was there.

"She thinks it's my coffee," Slake told himself.

Slake did not hurry. A whole new contingent of coffee drinkers arrived and left while Slake drank his breakfast, dunked six pieces of sugar, and providently slipped two more in his pocket. When Slake left this eatery, he went out into the arcade a warmer boy and a boy less harassed by hunger pains. Indeed, for the moment, Slake felt relatively unharassed by anything at all.

A little further along, through the turnstiles and up some stairs, Slake found himself in an enormous enclosure—the main concourse of Grand Central Station. The large cold and exposed place made him remember and consider now the need to return to school. As he did, two really terrible feelings swept through him—one down from his throat and the other up from his knees. As the descending and ascending terrible feelings collided in his gut, Slake arrived at a point—not to go back. It wasn't a decision. It was a non-decision, a non-act. Slake simply stopped where he was, and though people pushed past him, surging up from the black gates of the New York Central trains, Slake only swayed or pivoted slightly when jostled. His eyes were fixed at a point, way up on the wall opposite him, where the most enormous screen he had ever seen showed a scene in full color of a magnificent waterfall, the foam and spray so wet and real that Slake felt it would splash down on him.

Slake stood that way a long, long time. But after a while—it may have been the uncomfortable position of his neck—he slowly lowered his head and returned to view the scene around him. The rush hour had passed and he moved without a crowd to guide him, without direction or purpose, and found himself in a bleak waiting room with rows of varnished oak benches, and only an occasional waiting person on each long bench. Slake sat down.

There was a newsstand catering to the needs of travelers—newspapers, magazines, candy bars, chewing gum, cough drops, cigarettes, plastic ducks, automobiles and airplanes, and countless other merchandise. Slake watched as people bought papers and cigarettes, and then he noticed something. When people rose to leave the benches and resume their journeys, some left their newspapers behind. "Then why did they buy them?" Slake inquired of himself. The answer did not come to him, but when a man, only a short way down the bench from Slake, arose and left his paper, Slake slid down the bench and acquired it. At first he just stared at it, not really reading. Then he folded it, put it under his arm, and started to walk slowly and unobtrusively into the next aisle of seats. There was no paper there, but there was one in the next aisle. The next paper Slake picked up had a lady's glove in it. He held it, looked at it, and then, not knowing what else to do, put it back in the newspaper. In the corner of one bench Slake found a box of cough drops with one cough drop in it. He took that too. He did not know exactly why he was doing this, but Slake had learned early in life that if something is being cast out, acquire it, and determine its use at some other time. With this principle in mind, Slake acquired four copies of *The Daily News* and three copies of *The New York Times* after he had walked past all the benches in the waiting room twice. He also had three buttons, a pencil, and the head of a plastic doll. Slake put the last items in his pocket and then sat down and carefully smoothed and folded the newspapers. When he found the glove again, he put it on his left hand. Then he got up and started walking back through the passage to the subways.

Before he had gone fifty feet a man, rushing by, grabbed him by the shoulder, stopping him. Slake froze with fear.

"*News!*" snapped the man. Slake only stared. "*News*, boy!" And without waiting, he grabbed one of Slake's papers, slapped the money into his hand, and hurried on. Slake turned and stared after him. Then he drew in his breath sharply. Though inexperienced, he was not stupid. *Slake knew he was in business.*

Slake now walked with intent towards the part of the subway from which he had earlier emerged. He stood near the turnstiles, keeping a nervous eye on the change-booth attendant. When the man was involved in a transaction, Slake bent down as if to pick something up and slipped under the turnstile. It frightened him to do it. Slake committed crimes no more easily than he performed approved acts of living. He

31

descended the flight of stairs that took him to the uptown platform, and with hesitancy and fear, heart beating in his ears, Slake walked up and down conspicuously. People, leaning against blue pillars, stared straight ahead, or paced impatiently while waiting for their trains.

"They don't see me," Slake told himself, wishing this time to be visible.

And then a man who appeared to be looking at nothing at all finally focused on Slake.

"Hey, paper?" said Slake, the words pitched at a level and tone that made Slake wonder if they had been heard except in his own head, or even if they had really been uttered.

The man tilted his head. "What's that?" he asked.

"Paper," said Slake, now projecting. And his voice came out so unexpectedly loud that several people turned.

The man said, "No, thanks," but another man came across the platform.

"I'll have a *Times*," he said, and handed Slake the coins. Slake gave him a paper. With the fifteen cents he had just gotten for the *News*, that made thirty cents and no sweat!

A train came in and the scene changed. The station emptied suddenly like a sink with the plug pulled out. Slake stood quietly, shivering only occasionally as a draft came through the tunnel. Otherwise it was not unduly cold for November. The people traveling the trains did not seem especially bundled up nor red-faced and teary-eyed as they would become as the winter progressed. It was a gift of mild weather before the icy months.

Now the station started to fill; the blue pillars again supported leaners. A young boy tested his mother's tolerance by seeing how close he could stand to the yellow line at the edge of the station platform. Three working girls laughed wildly about some secret.

Slake cleared his throat and tried his voice again.

"Paper?"

The girls looked at him with absentminded blinks, and then one said to him, "You better keep an eye out for the transit cops. I never saw anyone peddling papers down here." And then she turned away and picked up her laugh where she'd left it.

"Well, look at that; a paper!" a man said. And he pushed the money into Slake's hand and took a copy of the *News*. Paper was the magic word down here.

When the next local arrived, Slake—dazed with his success and easy fortune—followed the people onto the train. He had no particular aim. Riders who had just boarded the train burrowed out spaces for themselves to sit in, or stood gripping straps that then began to manipulate them like marionettes—lean back, lean forward, lean back. . . . Slake, however, stood close to the doors, and suddenly a man sitting in the end seat signaled him. Slake drew back.

"Paper!" the man said and pushed a quarter into Slake's hand. Slake panicked. Which paper did the man want? He handed the quarter back, shaking his head. He'd have to make change.

"The *Times*," the man said with some impatience.

Slake managed to find a dime in his pocket. That had been an unexpected and exhausting transaction. He got off at Fifty-ninth Street in a hurry.

Weary now from this tense and unusual venture into the world of commerce, Slake wished to go out of business for the time being. He looked at his remaining papers. One was a bit torn, but the others were okay. . . . No, he'd had it, and besides, he had a plan for them. He slipped the remaining papers under his shirt, crossed to the downtown side, and when the train came in, Slake was on it. This time he knew where he was going.

Slake got off at Grand Central. First he went up the stairs and, near the toll booths, he purchased a Nestlé's Crunch for ten cents. Then he went back down the same flight of stairs to the downtown platform. Down the long platform

Slake walked until he had reached the end away from the dispatcher's office. Quickly slipping down the stairs, he waited quietly until a train came and went, assuring him that the track would be clear for a few minutes. Then he slid under the edge of the platform and made his way down the track and into the tunnel. He felt around cautiously for the entrance to the room he had occupied the night before. He panicked for just a moment when he could not find it. And then it was there. Through the hole he went. Slake was home.

He got busy immediately, not waiting for his eyes to adjust to the darkness. He took the newspapers from under his shirt and, sheet by sheet, he began to crumple them into soft, loose wads. He put about thirty of these close together in a corner of the room. He laid a couple of the loose pieces of timber around them to keep them from scattering. Then he covered them with three double sheets of newspaper. Slake had a bed.

Now he folded several pieces of the *News* and put them under his shirt again, front and back. He wrapped two other sheets around his arms and tied them with his shoelaces. Then he sat down on his bed and rested from his labors. After a few minutes he reached into his pocket and removed the two lumps of sugar from this morning's coffee, the cough drop, and the candy bar. Slake was hungry but not more so than he had been many times.

It was now that Slake found himself firmly committed to settling on this frontier. It never crossed his mind that life could not be sustained in the subway, but had there been a question, the answer would have been easy for him. Slake knew that life was some persistent weed that grew in gravel, in broken sidewalks, in fetid alleys, and would have no more difficulty doing so here than anywhere he knew.

ON ANOTHER TRACK

The idea of becoming a sheephand in Australia did not really leave Willis Joe. Sometimes he would walk down the street, playing a game he liked to play—looking in windows of stores and choosing the thing he would take if he were allowed to have the one thing he liked best. There were windows full of watches, and musical instruments, and tools, but there was nothing that appealed to him as much as the wide-brimmed hat he thought he might wear when he was riding his horse around in Australia. And the idea stayed with him even when his friends left school and went to work in factories, or in garages, or offices in Astoria, or in Long Island City, or in Manhattan, or Brooklyn.

Every other summer his mother took him to her old home in Iowa for a short vacation with his grandmother. Willis Joe looked forward to those trips in a Greyhound bus. He liked his grandmother. And then one time she had asked him what he wanted to be when he grew up and he had told her. When it was finally put into words the idea was much more real.

"A sheephand!" his grandmother had laughed. "Boy, I once knew a man who worked on a sheep ranch in Montana, and you couldn't tell him from a sheep the way he smelled. Listen, once when he was being a little too friendly

I told him so, too. And you know what he said to me?"

Willis Joe asked with real interest what the man had said.

"Well, he laughed and he said to me . . ." His grandmother now made her voice gruff. "He said, 'The difference between me and a sheep, ma'am, is that I've got a soul.' " His grand-mother's voice returned to normal. "That's what he said—*he* had a soul. Well, maybe so, but it wasn't enough, I'll tell you that."

And that was the only living person Willis Joe ever told about his idea.

There came a kind of order to Slake's life. He awoke at a regular time—a habit born of the fact that business hours were short and brisk early in the morning.

After that first day he did not return to the waiting room for newspapers because it was through the turnstiles. But he quickly found other sources of supply. He usually began his day by going down to the lowest level of the subway and riding the Flushing train to Times Square and back, systematically clearing it of newspapers which the passengers had read on the long trip in from Queens. He smoothed and folded them on the return trip and then climbed the stairs that took him back to the IRT and onto the uptown platform.

Another good source of supply was the waste baskets near the turnstile. Perfectly good newspapers were thrown in here in quantity, but there was no place to smooth them nicely and fold them, and Slake preferred to ride the train.

Within a week he had two regular customers on the uptown platform, and several irregular ones. One regular was a tall, turbaned man who grinned every time he gave Slake the money, as if (Slake thought) it were the man himself who was doing something dishonest. Because Slake had not overcome the feeling that he was, in fact, cheating his customers—selling secondhand papers at brand-new prices. But, he told himself, he had not started the business—someone had asked to buy. Two people had asked to buy. Was that *his* fault?

The second regular customer was a round lady in a longish coat and a wool hat pulled low over a smooth pink face. She took a very long time going through a bulging handbag for the change, and usually found it in pennies scattered all over the bottom of the bag. While she searched she held a one-way conversation with Slake—on the progress of her hunt for change, on the weather, on the state of life in general and on her small family in particular. For the most part it was cheerful and had the effect of a radio with the volume turned down.

After business hours of his second full day in the newspaper business, Slake had $1.35, counting some change he had found. When the last paper was sold, Slake made his way back to the lunch counter at which he had had coffee the day before. He was nervous about entering, but hunger pushed him forward. He ordered carefully, comparing the money in his pocket with the menu printed in large letters on a sign behind the counter. He decided on a bowl of vegetable soup and a ham sandwich. The soup was served with two wrapped packages of saltines. Slake put the saltines in his trouser pocket. Then he helped himself to a napkin and in it wrapped half of the sandwich and put it in his shirt pocket. Only then did he take a bite of the remaining half sandwich and a spoonful of hot soup. It was a luxurious meal. But Slake did not let comfort and wealth overwhelm him. He had to think ahead. He gathered all courage available to him and asked for something.

"What?" asked the waitress.

"Ketchup," said Slake.

"Ketchup! With ham!" The waitress laughed, but the truth is that she was used to any request and was not at all surprised. The ketchup came in little sealed plastic portions which Slake had seen on the serving counter. He put these in his pocket, and while he slowly ate his sandwich and sipped his soup, he also pocketed several cubes of sugar. Slake knew precisely what the food would cost—$1.05, plus tax. A lot of money. When the waitress put the check in front of him, he counted out the change carefully, put the exact amount on the counter, and quickly slid off the stool.

More comfortable in his stomach than he had been in recent memory, Slake was now ready to case his new neighborhood. He spent the next two hours in the underground passageways and arcades just getting his bearings.

His underground stomping grounds consisted of several levels. On the lowest level, sixty-five feet beneath the ground, was the platform of the

Flushing train, above which rose the great white vaulted ceiling. With its whitewashed walls, red and blue lines, yellow alcoves, this station was more like a circus than a subway. Beyond it, the great tunnel burrowed under the East River to Queens.

Above this level were the uptown and downtown platforms of the Lexington Avenue line. On the downtown side, Slake dwelled; on the uptown side, Slake worked. This station was not circus-like; indeed, it was dreary despite its blue pillars, but Slake's attention was caught by the little mosaic insets of locomotives repeated many times in the tile wall.

On the next level were the turnstiles, the token booth, the candy machine, and a small refreshment stand. Then began the long arcade to the shuttle, along which were shops of many kinds. There was the luncheonette where Slake had just eaten. There was a camera store, a newsstand, a florist, a jewelry shop, a shop that repaired watches, a clothing store, and several other shops including a shoeshine stand tended by a boy of about Slake's age. It was a city under the city . . . a city underneath the stones.

In his city beneath the city Slake saw trains passing, full of people, full of life. Going somewhere. Where? In his short escapes into the subway in the past, perhaps he had not gone far enough to find out. It was then that Slake decided to spend the major part of his afternoons on subway excursions. The first several trips were haphazard. He merely went where the train took him, transferred as the mood possessed him. He let the subway lead him.

But later Slake took over. He developed a grand plan of exploration. Carefully studying the large subway map on the wall of the train, he divided the city into portions—its five natural boroughs and within them, divisions within divisions. And during the course of his stay in the subway, Slake managed to explore systematically every inch of the hundred and thirty-seven miles that ran underground, and by his own tally which he kept with him he stopped at every one of the two hundred and sixty-five underground stations. But he would not travel to the elevated stations which would take him above ground, so it might have to be said that his tour was incomplete.

Sometimes Slake rode just looking out of a window as if there were sights to be seen on the dark concrete walls. And his familiarity with the subway became so sensitive that his inner timing system would tell him when a station was being approached and what station it was.

But often he would ride standing at the very

front of the first car, right next to the motorman's door, watching the tracks twisting across each other, keeping an eye out for green lights giving clearance, watching yellow lights announce caution, then waiting for clearance at the next signal. At a junction Slake would read the double sets of signs—yellow over red, red over yellow. He began to know the signs of the subway as a woodsman knows the wilderness—signs along the tracks announcing curves or descent, signs signaling the motorman to curb speed. Men working along the tracks flashed lights and waved flags and the motorman responded with the train whistle. Slake watched trains coming on another track towards him, watched the crocodile of a third rail giving off sparks, its tail disappearing around the curve. Thus did Slake discover America—a subterranean Henry Hudson.

Slake spent considerable time reading the messages of the subway. The word was on the wall . . . and large so that Slake could read it without difficulty. A dweller in the subway need have no library, carry no book. In bright spray paint and felt pen the walls of the subway cars were inscribed with thousands of names and messages. Zip 168, Big Man, Louie 125, Augie II, Hum Bug, Pee Wee. But in between, and most particularly on the walls of the stations,

Slake read innumerable interesting communications. There were statements and often replies.

GOD LIVES
Good Lives
Good God!

LOUSY!   LOUSY!!   LOUSY!!!

Where is Smitty?
IN THE CAN.

HELP!

Strike, STRIKE, STRIKE

A RAT BITE ME
Bite it back

PEACE!

Panik button. Push

I GOT NO TIME LEFT

Slake wished to write a message too, but at first he lacked the means, and he lacked the nerve always. One message Slake liked said:

SAVE THE WORLD FOR
BENNY POMERANTZ

At the end of the day's excursion when he sensed the rush hour coming on, Slake threaded his way through the caverns until the train deposited him at Grand Central once again. He returned with a sense of belonging, but he remained very cautious in making his way back to his cave. First he would go to the far end of the platform, away from the dispatcher's office, ducking under the edge of the platform after a train had passed, and make his way to the other end of the station unseen. Then came the tightrope walk along the third rail to the cave, over and in, and Slake was home again.

Slake worried about being seen sneaking to the platform edge and down the stairs. But he became so adept that on only two occasions was he really noticed. The first was by a small girl who had wandered down the platform and stood staring at Slake as he held to the wall near the bottom of the steps.

"Watcha doin'?" the girl asked.

"Workin'," Slake said, bending down and disappearing under the edge of the platform.

On the other occasion, a man pacing the length of the platform while waiting for a delayed number four train, saw Slake going down the track stairs.

"Hey there!" he called, and since Slake did not stop, he turned and pointed and gestured. "Where's that kid going?" he asked nobody who could hear him. By the time the man had paced back to the peopled section of the station, Slake was well under the platform edge and heading for the other end of the station and the safety of his cave.

And then one late afternoon, making his way home, Slake found a treasure under the platform—two battery lanterns left by the track crew. He did not hesitate. He acquired them. From then on the cave was lit.

When Slake sat down to dine in the evening, his dinner awaited him in his shirt pocket—the second half of his lunch sandwich. It was not lavish but enough to sustain life—thick slices of soft bread, somewhat mashed from his pocket, a fair slice of ham, and a piece of wilted lettuce. And Slake had not overlooked a most important thing—water. He had been acquiring many useful items through salvage, and among these were some used Coca-Cola cans. He had rinsed these out in the washroom and kept them filled. And Slake was beginning to develop ideas about how to use some of the other odds and ends he collected.

In his whole life before this Slake had never had a room of his own—indeed, he had never had a room, just the kitchen. No room, except once there had been a pigeon coop that he could remember on the roof of a building where he had once lived. There above the streets, in his nearly forgotten young afternoons, he had spent many hours out of reach of the flailing arms of his classmates and the voice of the aunt.

Now beneath the streets, he luxuriated in the privacy of a room of his own. Slake reached for his cool can of water and washed down his sandwich.

In Slake's past, the aunt had been an overwhelming presence. Once she had given Slake a bag of bottles to return to the grocery for the deposit. Slake knew he would not get to the grocery with the bottles. How did Slake know? He knew because he knew. Halfway there he was set upon by three boys who helped themselves to the bottles, and Slake returned to the flat without the deposit money.

The aunt had set upon him. First she had cried, "Liar!" and searched him. Then she accused him of buying some candy with the money. Then, when she was convinced that he had not had time to get to the store and back to buy and consume the candy, she had set upon him again for his carelessness and puniness. Slake's expectations for good were not great . . . were not great . . . were not. . . .

6 Slake now began to feel a sense of responsibility to his two regular customers
and even to several irregular ones. He
felt that the pink-faced lady and the man
with the turban had come to rely on him for their
papers. He tried to serve them first, although he
soon began to develop a nervousness when the
man with the turban approached.

The pink-faced lady was counting out money.
"There's one . . . ," she said, capturing a
penny. "There's two . . . ," in the lining of the
bag. "I know I have a bunch of pennies in here
because I threw them in last night. Picked 'em
up in the sofa cushions. Do you know pennies
fall into sofa cushions more than dimes? Why is
that?" Slake didn't know why.

"When my son comes to visit, they fall out of
his pocket all the time. Why does he always have
so many pennies?"

Slake didn't know that either, but it was like a
story that came out bit by bit with the money.
The pink-faced lady had a son who came to visit
her often and whenever he sat on the sofa pennies fell out of his pocket. Was this son careless?
Did he have holes in his pockets? Slake found
himself wondering about the son. What did he
do? Where did he live? How was it that he came
to see his mother so often?

"You know," the lady said to Slake one day
while she fished for change, "it's not right for it

49

to be so dangerous down here in the subway. A person doesn't feel safe at all anymore, day or night. I'll tell you I am scared. Why the person standing next to you who looks perfectly nice might mug you or steal your purse . . . even kill you. There was a woman pushed right off the platform a few months ago, just a few minutes before I got here. There was a man knifed! You watch out, hear!"

Slake did not really understand why she said all that. Were these not the very same people in the subway who walked on the street above? And how were the things she was describing any different than the things Slake knew above ground? But she had no need to warn Slake; he had spent his whole life watching out. At night Slake was well away in his cave, out of the way of civilization . . . out of the way of the moving mountains of boys who charged into the subway, loud and looming walls of flesh, crashing and echoing in the subway, high on wine or potent potions, coming, perhaps, to decorate the walls of the subways with their spray cans, to write their messages and monuments to themselves. No need to tell Slake to watch out; he watched out for everything hostile, and anything outside Slake's skin had been hostile till now, and a great deal inside of it as well.

"And that's fourteen," the lady was saying.

"Whoops! There's my train! Just in time!" And she waved a cheerful goodbye to Slake. "I owe you a penny," she called, rushing for the door. "I'll give it to you tomorrow."

And the next day she did, and only had to fish for six pennies because she found a dime first.

"There, that's three," she said, ". . . and four. No, that's a button from my son's coat. It must have fallen into the sofa with the change."

Did her son come every night, then? The answer came in time—he visited her on his bowling nights. She gave him dinner.

"And that's sixteen cents. Aren't you cold?"

Slake shook his head and handed her the paper, looking at her from the side and beneath his eyes in a way that gave him a feeling that he was unobserved while observing.

"My, this is really handy getting the paper like this," said the lady, as a man came up and shoved money at Slake and grabbed a paper from under his arm. "It's like being waited on, you know, getting my paper while I wait here. I'm not used to service. Not at all. On the contrary," she laughed, "I'm used to giving it. I tidy the house of a gentleman uptown. Done the same thing for years. Have to get up early, but I'm through work by noon. That's the good part of it. I always try to look for the good part."

Slake nodded. He had never known so much

about any stranger before and in Slake's life everyone was a stranger and none were known . . . except Joseph. But now strangers began to fall into two groups—known strangers and unknown strangers. The known strangers were this cleaning lady, the waitress at the luncheonette where he was now a regular customer, and even, perhaps, the man with the turban.

But Slake had begun to fear this man because of his secret smile, and because of the feeling that the man was cheating him of something—confidence—and Slake had so little to be cheated of that not a centimeter could be lost without fear.

One day, seeing the man approaching with the strange and secret smile, Slake had felt panic and turned away, wishing himself invisible. He stared at the track and stared at the track.

"What you looking for, son?" It was the man's clipped accent. Slake had hunched his head down into his shoulders, closing his eyes so that he could see nothing and, it was his hope, hear nothing.

"What say, son?"

Slake tried and gritted out the word, "Nothin'."

"Oh," the man said. "Then, you're sure to find it. You going to sell me a paper, eh?" And Slake did, but he managed not to look at the man.

As the days passed, the anxious feeling that Slake developed about the man with the turban made him think that he might have to change the time that he came to this platform. But then he would not be able to sell his paper to the cleaning lady and to the other people who occasionally bought a paper from him. Slake had begun to find a certain comfort in the routine. It had produced no real problems except for the man with the turban.

Then, on a day that he saw the man coming toward him, Slake turned and tried to walk casually to the other end of the station. But the man's long legs reached him without changing their pace.

"Paper, please." And Slake had to turn and reach under his arm for the paper. He held it out without looking up. It was not taken, nor did the change come dropping into his palm as usual. But the man spoke conversationally as if he had all the time there was, and there was no train to catch.

"Say, boy, where do you get these papers, eh?"

That was it! The man was going to put him out of business. He had been found out!

"The trains." Slake answered a direct question with a direct answer and was surprised at how easy it was.

"Ah," said the man, dropping the money into Slake's palm, and turned and walked down the platform again. What would the man do?

Slake sweated all night, though the little room was not hot. He stayed in his cave all the following morning and did not go for papers. When he went out later in the afternoon, he rode the shuttle without much enthusiasm, and picked up a few papers in pretty bad shape, sat-on and torn. Slake did not have the money for his meal that day. He stayed on the West Side and rode the BMT down to City Hall and back again, his planned itinerary forgotten. He felt, somehow, cast adrift.

Late that afternoon he returned to his cave to sup on water and to read one of the newspapers that made up his bed, which he regularly replaced as they flattened and lost their buoyancy. Lantern-lit, the cave was quite homey, and Slake relaxed on his bed to read, holding the paper close to his face, and his face close to the lantern. His attention was caught time and time again by photographs of fallen victims of crime, or villains caught by bullets, lying in a bath of their own blood. It was not that this was a totally strange sight to Slake. In the days of his years he had seen people lying in blood. What struck him was that, in black and white, blood did not look like much. It did not seem real, and so he read the stories surrounding the pictures as just more fantasies of the printed page.

These, and the stories of big-bellied, stick-legged children wiped out by thousands in an epidemic, in some unpronounceable country, were not unlike the kind of scary stories that teachers used to read out loud sometimes in elementary school—only vaguely terrifying because, even then, Slake had known the stories could not be true. He knew the real terrors were not man-eating giants, mean dwarfs, or wicked witches, but big tough fellows on his block or in his class, sometimes carrying small sharp knives in their shoes, always having heavy knuckled fists like snowballs packed with stones. The only one of the stories at school that had really frightened Slake was about children lost in the woods and starving, because there was one thing Slake knew—he knew truth. He knew fact from fiction.

When Slake awoke the next morning, the bird which had been only a vague presence in his chest of late, was crying piteously. Slake sipped water for his breakfast and took the Flushing train to the Times Square station to collect his papers. He wished not to go, but something drew him to the platform.

The pink cleaning lady smiled. "Say, I worried

about you yesterday. And I missed my paper. Were you sick? Here I have the money all ready, see."

Slake felt strange. He was shaking. "Don't tell me you're not cold," the lady said severely.

He wasn't cold; he was frightened. The man with the turban was approaching. He was like the mob at school. Slake was a whole block of fear. Had fear followed him here or had they arrived together? Now he wished to return to his cave and hide, but it was too late.

"Five cents!" Slake said thinly and thrust the paper at the man with the turban.

"Why five?" asked the man, after a pause, and he said it calmly but seriously.

"Secondhand," whispered Slake, pushing the paper at him, and looking nervously over his shoulder.

"Oh, I know that," said the man, "but it's worth it to me not to have to stop at the newsstand. And you smooth them out real well. You deliver. You're charging for service. That's fair enough."

Slake was stunned, but his curiosity was now so strong that his voice took over in spite of him.

"Whyd'ya chase me, then?" he heard his hoarse voice asking.

"Chase you!" The man laughed his deep laugh. "When did I chase you?"

Slake could not find the sound in his throat

again. But I was running, he thought to himself, so he must have been chasing me.

The man looked at Slake's silent worried face. "Look, boy, I want a paper, but not bad enough to chase after it." The man laughed again, and then he gave Slake a pat on the shoulder and turned to catch the train.

ON ANOTHER TRACK

Just before he was eighteen, Willis Joe Whinny's star fell, but he did not know that then. Before Christmas, that year, Willis Joe's father slipped on the ice and broke his hip. It was going to be a long time before he could do any heavy work again and Willis Joe left school to help out. He got a job sweeping up and generally working around a garage near his house in Astoria. Then he started to service cars and by and by he began to learn things about becoming a mechanic.

He was doing okay, but after a few years, his uncle suggested that Willis Joe try to get a job like he had with the subway. "You'll get more money and then, when you're ready to retire, you get that nice pension from the city." Willis Joe had not started to think about retiring. He was just thinking about getting started, but he managed to get a job as a conductor on the subway. He thought he'd be able to save up some money for the long trip to Australia.

In six months Willis Joe passed the test to become a motorman and as soon as he got off the extra sheet—filling in for motormen who were out sick or on vacation—he was allowed to pick his own route and was able to work out of the Ditmars Boulevard terminal, which wasn't far from his home. And then pretty soon he began to think about how reassuring it was that, when he got ready to retire, there was that pension. . . .

He married a really nice girl named Lily, and they had two children, Joe and Wilma.

Australia was farther away than it used to be.

7 The next day when Slake gave the cleaning lady her paper, she handed him a large, brown paper bag.

"Now, it's just something of my son's that doesn't fit him anymore, and if you can use it, good. If you can't, you just give it away." Slake's hand accepted the bag. "And there'll be a pair of jeans when I'm done mending 'em."

The bag contained a zippered jacket. It was of some brown slippery fabric that was quilted and puffy. While the lady was waiting for her train, Slake just held the jacket and stared at her and shook his head slowly in both directions, and then tried his voice.

"Thanks." But he wasn't sure that he'd actually uttered it. It wasn't until the lady boarded the train that Slake put the jacket on. It was a few sizes too big, but that didn't trouble him.

When Slake, with warm jacket on and a newspaper under his arm, went to lunch, he was nearly but not quite able to meet the eye of the waitress who put before him his daily meal. While waiting for his lunch, Slake investigated the jacket. It had two good pockets—great places to put the half-sandwich he regularly saved for his dinner, the package of saltines, and the pieces of sugar.

Now here was another odd thing. For quite a while the counter girl had been putting more in front of him than he ordered. There might be three packages of saltines with his soup, and some celery or carrot or pickle or other salad bits beside his sandwich. There might be a bunch of potato chips. The lettuce was thick on the sandwich. Sometimes she seemed to misunderstand and give him ham and egg instead of ham. Slake thought about this. He was, after all, ordering only what he regularly ordered and paying the same price for the food. If the girl made mistakes and gave him hamburger plate when he asked for a ham sandwich, and only charged him for the sandwich, that wasn't his fault. Was it? He looked at her out of the corner of his eye. She was short, and of no particular age, and freckled, and knobby here and there, and perhaps a bit tubby, and stubby-fingered, and bunchy-haired, and in her own way quite roughly wonderful.

What feeling caused the counter girl to move food in the direction of Slake's stomach? Pity? Slake's experience did not include pity given or received, and so he would not have recognized it if it were this. But Slake did recognize in this act something he knew only slightly, passingly—not so much the presence of something as the absence of something.

The things Slake pocketed ended up in the late afternoon in his cave pantry where he laid out his dinner on a table made of a discarded cardboard carton. In the course of time Slake's cave had acquired not only added function but decor, because besides becoming a seller of newspapers and an expert subway traveler, Slake by this time had become an excellent scavenger. Nothing that could be used as it was or turned into something else escaped Slake's notice, and he turned up such a surprising amount of trash, truck, and treasure, including useful, somewhat useful, and possibly useful things, that eventually he was able to become selective. He brought back, to his home under the Commodore, more than even he could imagine a use for, and eventually he found himself in the magnificent position of being able to throw things away. Every day he brought things in, and every day he took out a newspaper parcel full of his own discards and deposited it with a sense of extravagance in the subway trash can, perhaps for someone more needy than he to reclaim.

Slake did his scavenging with a shopping bag which the trash can had produced. Into this went string, wire, wire hangers, paper clips, broken buckles, shoelaces, rubber bands, and countless other things that could be made into lacings, hooks, hinges to help in the construction of articles functional and decorative.

One side of the room became a storage place and Slake, who had never before had a place to keep anything nor owned anything much to keep, now spent several hours a day sorting and storing things, seeing what they may have been and what, combined with something else, they might become. He organized, reorganized, discarded, and eventually achieved fairly neat piles of possessions that he classified as follows:

Glass things. There were broken or cracked mirrors, aspirin and liquor bottles, several lenses from eyeglasses, colored glass beads from ill-fated necklaces, and a broken drinking glass. The mirrors served as mirrors; the bottles were used to hold the glass beads and other items, and even to preserve a faded pink carnation, fallen from the buttonhole of some homeward-bound floor manager. Even the lenses turned out to have a use.

Paper things. There were bags, smoothed and stacked, paper napkins from the coffee shop, extra newspapers for bedding and wrapping, magazines for reading and for tearing out pictures, and paper cups. Cardboard cartons, discarded early in the morning by the stores, became Slake's furniture and storage bins.

Metal things. Hairpins and bobby pins were the most common and Slake bent and twisted these together to make hooks or lengths of wire. Keys abounded too, and in time Slake strung a bunch of these together and wore them tied to a loop on his belt. There were wire hangers, the bottom half of an old tin box, ribs from a broken umbrella, a brass shoe buckle, bits of wire from packing crates, and a number of large nuts and bolts that were found on the track. Most valuable of these was the broken blade of a pocketknife which became Slake's main tool for transforming his things into other things.

Art things. He had ten nearly empty cans of spray paint in a great many colors, and a good selection of marking pens and pencils. His most valuable thing was an adhesive which he had mixed himself. Its main ingredients were chewing gum and the heavy tar-like grease which accumulated on the side of the track. Slake's glue held things together splendidly and also mended things with holes.

Clothes. This collection had started with the glove Slake found the first day (and which he later joined with hairpins to the doll's head to form a hand puppet). He found many more single gloves and mittens, giving him a large wardrobe of mismatched hand warmers, and there were several scarfs and broken belts and two hats. One was a flat-billed cap, which fit Slake quite well. There was also, for a while, one shoe. But this bothered Slake because he pondered the question of its foot. He eventually discarded it.

Everything else. This included buttons of all sizes and shapes, earrings, string, matches, heels from shoes, plastic forks and spoons, two tubes of lipstick, and three empty leather wallets.

While sorting through his collection one day, Slake heard sounds in the tunnel—clinking, low talking, occasional shouts, then a train passing, then more sounds. It was near; too near! The bird in Slake started pecking at his ribs. Slake identified the sounds—clink, clink, drag. He'd heard them before; a track crew maintaining the line, cleaning it of debris, testing this bolt and that rail. They would find him! He tried to tell himself that this hole had been here a long time. They had overlooked it before; they would not find it now . . . not if he did not move, did not breathe. He stood quietly poised, like a crane. They would not see it! But as the clinking sounds came closer, Slake grabbed a piece of cardboard from his supply of papers and put it across the hole. He leaned on the cardboard, sealing himself in like a jack-in-the-box, like a clam in a shell. Though his room was chilly, he sweated. How long did it take to fix a length of track? Too long. Slake felt weak when they had passed. He fell onto his bed and curled up in a way that allowed as little of himself as possible to be exposed to the world.

That was the day Slake found a pair of broken eyeglasses. One earpiece was missing and both lenses were smashed. When he returned to his cave, Slake tried on the frames. He regarded himself in the mirror which he had put together on the floor from bits of broken mirrors. He looked fragmented. He pushed out the broken lenses and sorted through his accumulation of odd lenses until he located two that seemed to do his eyes the most good—not perfect, but better. He then proceeded to attach them to the frame. He scooped up some of his homemade adhesive and stuck it into the grooves of the frame. Then he fitted, as best he could, the glass to the groove, bending the frame here and there. Except for a crack and some scratches one lens was usable and fit the frame quite well. The other lens was tinted a light pink and had only a chip out of the top; a pretty good lens and it seemed to improve his normal vision. However, it stuck way up over the top of the frame, so he fixed its position firmly with a piece of wire that bisected his vision. Though it broke up the sights around him, the effect brightened and sharpened Slake's world.

His customers noticed.

"Oh, my!" said the cleaning lady. "I hadn't realized you wore glasses. What an unusual pair!" Slake ducked his head.

"Say, son!" said the man with the turban. "What do you call those shades? I never did see a pair like that." He peered at Slake closely, bending and looking directly into his eyes. "Do they really work?"

Slake nodded.

"Good enough!" the man said and turned away.

Good enough. Slake wondered now what had frightened him about this man. "Good enough," Slake found himself saying as he walked along. Good enough was good enough.

3 Slake's breakfast consisted of the cubes of sugar which he cadged daily, and the saltines liberally spread with ketchup. This and his luncheonette meal, which was extended to cover his supper, was his total food intake. No one would say it was a balanced diet. But Slake had never been subjected to the benefits of a balanced diet. Scurvy, rickets, iron deficiency anemia, calcium lacks, vitamin and mineral imbalances had always been unimportant compared to the more important objective— filling the void in his middle. And then things became suddenly better.

It was during the Christmas rush. The subway, always teeming, now seemed that it would burst with humanity. The coffee shop was busier than ever. Slake was having his meal of the day when the man who seemed to be in charge spoke to him.

"I see you here every day."

Slake took fright. Did he know the waitress was giving him extras?

"Do you want a job?" Slake looked up. "Tell you what; if you want, you come in after the morning rush and sweep up the floor for me, and I'll give you a good meal. How's that for a business proposition?" Slake nodded. "Good," the man said as he rushed to serve another customer. "I've got just too much to do to do everything."

Slake had entered into his first contract without saying a word or signing his name. Every morning after selling his newspapers, he turned up at the coffee shop and silently took up the broom and swept. He swept like someone planning to learn the art and make it a life work. He got every crumb from under every stool, from every corner. He bent down and pushed the broom under the counter edge and hunted out wadded paper napkins, soda straws, cigarette butts, matches, and all kinds of trash. And he found forty cents in change the very first day.

"What you find, you keep," said the manager. "You sweep good. Real good!"

When had someone said that to Slake before? Sometime. He remembered it; run. Run! That was it. Someone had said, "You run good. Real good." And now he also "swept good." To run, to sweep; what else might he do!

"What'll you eat?" the waitress asked him the first day he worked.

Slake spoke slowly. He was puzzled. He thought she knew his order by now. She never asked him anymore. "Soup and ham sandwich," he said.

She put the soup in front of Slake and then she served a big hamburger on a bun surrounded by french fried potatoes and a tomato. And when Slake thought he was through, she brought him a wedge of apple pie with a lump of vanilla ice

69

cream on it. When Slake started to cut the hamburger in half as he always did to save for his supper, she said, "Don't bother," and she put a wrapped sandwich beside him.

Slake took a long time over lunch. He did not know when he had had so much food. When he got down from the stool, the feeling of fullness was so palpable that he nearly lost his balance.

In his pocket was the extra sandwich, the ketchup packets, the saltines, the sugar. Slake looked at the manager and he struggled for the word and found it. "Thanks," he said, and he nearly looked at the waitress too, so the one word served them both.

The next day he took a wet mop from the corner and got some stubborn spots up from the floor. The floor and its condition became his special concern. He even thought that since he started to tend it, it was immeasurably improved. The manager obviously thought so too. After that no one asked Slake what he wanted to eat. Lunch, often a hot stew or whatever the special of the day might be, was set before him. And when he left, the waitress handed him a small bag which turned out to hold his next two meals—sweet crackers or a donut, a sandwich, an apple or orange, a container of milk. Slake had never been so well tended.

With the free meals, Slake began to accumulate some money in his pockets, and when some of it began to take the form of paper money, Slake selected, from his collection of things, a brown wallet with fancy stitches on its edges. Although Slake continued to be distressed by the necessity of making change, having the wallet made it somehow more tolerable. In time it became full enough for him to purcase a T-shirt, two pairs of socks and shorts from a clothing shop in the arcade, and then he began saving for some new sneakers. Slake felt, in fact, that he had a rather fine wardrobe with the jeans that the cleaning lady had brought one day.

So now Slake was a vender of papers, a custodian of a small thriving coffee shop, and a discriminating scavenger. And he was also a hobbyist. Above ground, in the chambers of the hotel, for instance, there were probably some people who pursued similar hobbies and called it collecting—collage, montage, abstract art. . . .

From the materials that Slake acquired while prowling the corners of the station, the edges of the track, the car seats, and all the recesses of the subway, he fashioned objects that were purely ornamental and decorative. Slake's home— Slake's cave, Slake's castle, Slake's haven—was now decorated, hung, festooned with ornaments of his own creation which, when lit by lantern light, made the place entirely gala. Mobiles made of wire hangers were suspended from

71

string stuck to the ceiling with Slake's chewing gum adhesive. They were balanced just so with colored pieces of paper, buttons, hairpin figures, glass beads, and fragments of mirrors, catching the light and casting their vague shapes and shadows on the wall.

During the Christmas shopping season, people carrying packages moved as if they were on a never-ending belt of a machine that couldn't stop. Round and round these people and packages went, crisscrossing, ducking under, dodging around. Slake managed to salvage a good deal of very interesting fallout from this friction of people and packages. He had any number of bright package trimmings that had toppled off in the crush—gold tassels, stars and pom-poms, bits of gold and red string, and loops of foil. By Christmas day he had such a collection that he replaced his regular display of mobiles with a seasonal exhibition. With the lanterns throwing their light on the holiday creations, Slake had himself quite a Christmas—the best ever. The luncheonette had closed for the holiday, but the waitress had packed him enough to tide him over. There were several sandwiches, two tomatoes, apples, and a big piece of raisin-filled pound cake.

Slake took his ease, moving a lantern here or a lantern there to change the play of light on the swaying mobiles—figures of his hands and mind. They caught the light and played out entertainments for Slake. They cast their shadows and so played twice—once sharply and brightly, once darkly and softly.

That was Christmas in the subway—the subway with its passages to everywhere.

ON ANOTHER TRACK

At some point Willis Joe started to drive his train as if he were riding a horse and herding sheep. This transformation started at an exact spot—the stretch of track between 138th and 149th Streets on the IRT where a roughness in the track set up a bumping motion in the train that suggested the trotting gait of a horse. On his next trip to Woodlawn, Willis Joe experienced the same thing. He did not give it any thought, but the next day when he was driving an IND express train and could ride the long distance between the 59th and 125th Street stops at top speed with his brake handle in the multiple position, Willis Joe Whinny found that he was, indeed, enjoying the sensation of herding sheep in the wide-open Australian countryside. True, it was not just like Australia. The air was damp and cloistered. The tunnels obscured the sky most of the time. But after a very short while, Willis Joe had been able to cut through these difficulties and he herded sheep into pens for shearing, or drove them long distances to market.

To Willis Joe, red lights now meant whoa, and green meant giddup. He'd go with the woolies, ride the line, do the outriding. It was good . . . for a while.

9 Nearly every day Slake saw two people or more whom he knew, who recognized him and who did not hurt or threaten him. Indeed, they seemed to welcome him. But, having made this connection with the flow of humanity, Slake observed that there were many other human beings whom he encountered, who entered his sphere for just a few minutes and left, never to be seen again. What happened to them, Slake wondered. Where did they go? Once past Grand Central, did they get lost in the world? Were their travels so wide that there was not time to return to this spot once more, to stand again with people with whom they had passed the minutes waiting for the train? But the cleaning lady always returned, and the man with the turban, and some others came frequently, and Slake. Slake returned.

One day an elderly gentleman, dressed neatly in a mismatched way and limping badly, approached. He spoke to a very well-dressed man who was standing close to where Slake was just completing his paper sale to the cleaning lady.

"Pardon me, sir," the elderly gentleman said to the well-dressed man. "Do you know a baldheaded man with a cane who is at this stop about this time of the morning?"

The well-dressed man shook his head and said, "Sorry."

"Ah, that's too bad," the elderly gentleman

said. "I'm a doctor, you see, and I'm giving a lecture and demonstration tomorrow evening. Now, just the other day when we got to talking, this man with the cane had shown an interest in my work, and I wrote down his name and address." The elderly gentleman shook his head sadly, tut-tutting.

"I had promised to send him a notice of my lecture, you see," the doctor continued, "but now I've gone and lost the piece of paper I wrote the address on. I was hoping to run into him and tell him about the lecture myself. He seemed so very interested. I thought I could help him. Too bad. Too bad."

Suddenly the doctor spun on his heel so that he was very close to the well-dressed man. "Let me do something for you instead," he said, and before the other man could reply, the doctor had clamped his hand firmly on the man's shoulder, setting him off balance.

"By the grace of God and the power of my right hand, I now declare the rheumatism of this shoulder to be gone." He limped quickly to the man's other shoulder and grasped it. "By the grace of God and the power of my right hand, I now declare the rheumatism of this shoulder to be gone." Then he placed his hand on the man's rather round belly. "By the grace of God and the power of my right hand, I command your rupture to disappear. Turn around," and he attempted to spin the man completely around. But now the patient had recovered his balance and his senses.

"That's enough," he said, giving a firm push to the doctor. "That's enough!"

"God bless you," said the doctor, and he limped very quickly towards the stairs, never to be seen again.

The cleaning lady and Slake had been staring at the performance as at a school play. The show being over, the lady turned to leave the theater and board the train which was sliding into the station. The well-dressed man caught the cleaning lady's eye.

"After my wallet, I think," he said. He felt the wallet in his pocket. "I believe, now, that he was after my wallet!"

Slake wished to ask him how his rheumatism and his rupture were, but he did not.

At the busiest times of day, the surging and swelling of the crowds through the trains' double doors at the transfer points bothered Slake. He watched with a kind of breathless horror as a man fought to keep his feet while trying to gain a toehold in the train before the doors closed. The man would lean back against the crowd while a station guard tried to wedge him all the way into the car. Would the man be permitted to stay, or would the roiling crowd push him out once again onto the platform. It was often touch and go. And each time he saw it or experienced it, something tugged at Slake's memory.

It was when a man actually fell that he remembered. The man had made his way in, nearly achieved a permanent place, when the collective exhalation of breath or a unison lurch threw him out with such force that he fell on the platform. And then Slake remembered!

The ocean. A bus had taken him, through no choice of his own, with many other children to see the ocean. The ride was long and hot. Slake had been sick on the bus. Once at the shore, though, the great rolls of breaking waves charmed Slake. When he walked toward them, feeling the wet sand under his feet, he was quite hypnotized. Into the ocean he walked. And then the waves broke! They broke with such unexpected force that Slake could not understand it. Water was soft, he had thought. And then there was the swell of another wave. Was someone calling Slake? He turned and started to run, but that was so hard to do in the water. And then the arms of the great wave clutched at Slake. He stumbled and fell in the shallows and lay shivering there with the other flotsam.

Atlantic Avenue at 2:30 P.M. and Slake witnessed the takeover of an entire subway car by a group of high school boys, leaping, punching, laughing, wrestling, tightrope-walking on the seats, and finally pulling the emergency cord bringing the train to a sudden stop in the tunnel. Now the boys scrambled for seats and began to study books or stare ahead blankly.

In a minute the door between the cars was opened and the trainman came through. He surveyed the study hall.

"There some trouble, Mr. Conductor?" asked one of the youths.

"All right, you kids," the trainman said. And he sounded tired.

Slake had noticed that for some time the bird had not picked at his ribs very much. But now it was doing so, and as soon as the trainman had left, he got up and quickly opened the door between the cars and moved into the next car.

There were some stops Slake decided to avoid at certain hours. One of them was Atlantic Avenue when school let out.

10 When Slake retired for the night he performed a new ritual that added order to his life and comfort to his morning. He laid a fresh sheet of newspaper on the carton that served as his table, and on it he put his breakfast—the saltines, donut, orange or apple, or whatever tidbit the waitress had put in his bag that day. He took a can of water and set it beside these breakfast foods, and thus made ready a repast which, in the hotel beyond the wall, would be called a continental breakfast, served in his room, at that.

Early in Slake's stay, even before the richness of donuts and fruit were added, there appeared upon the scene another creature who also had an interest in Slake's breakfast foods. Slake awakened one day and let his eyes rove the walls of his home. He reached for his glasses and, as an incentive to rising, he glanced at his breakfast table. Slake blinked and looked again. He was absolutely sure of what he was seeing. He was seeing a small rat having his breakfast. Slake froze. Brought up in a world where one learned early to hate rats, he first felt a desire to scream and scare it away. But then, would it turn and attack him? Where Slake had lived, rats were known to attack. So he did nothing. He lay quietly and watched the rodent consume his breakfast. It seemed in a terrible hurry. It shredded the paper wrapping of the crackers. It ate as if it had not eaten in a very long time. And Slake observed that it was, indeed, a very thin rat— smaller by half than those he had seen running down alleys and in the littered back lots near his home. There was something limp and almost pathetic about this rat, and Slake thought it reminded him of something . . . but what? When it had consumed the crackers, it nosed about for something else. It found a crumb or two on the floor, perhaps from some other meal. Then it returned and extracted another crumb or so from the wrappings. And when there was nothing left, it turned and crossed to the entrance. Then, without looking back, it climbed up and out onto the tracks. Slake ran to the entrance but he could not see the rat anywhere. He returned to drink water and ketchup.

Slake decided not to go without breakfast again. That day he hunted through the trash baskets but he couldn't find anything suitable. And then he remembered the half of the tin box he'd found. It now held miscellaneous wires and buttons. He returned to his cave and dumped these into a paper bag. Then he put the tin box upside down over the food on his table. On this he put a fair-sized stone from the floor of his cave.

The next morning Slake was triumphant. He'd done it! His breakfast was undisturbed. No rat had been lured to a tin box anchored by a stone. Slake sat cross-legged before his table to start an undisturbed breakfast. Not so. He was just spreading the ketchup on the saltines when the rat materialized at the doorway. Had he been there all the time, just waiting? Slake grabbed his food and staked out his claim. The rat did not move; it simply stared at Slake. Okay, Slake thought, so it wasn't going to fight. Well, that was only right. No rat would hassle him for his breakfast. Slake relaxed. Though he was not pleased by its presence while he ate, he was interested in the rat's quiet vigil. When Slake rose and gathered up the papers, the rat turned and disappeared.

On the station that morning there was a new face—that of a very old woman. She was making her way down the platform. She stopped to talk with a few people as she made her way along. When she reached the cleaning lady, Slake found out what it was about.

"Dear," said the old woman waving a crumpled piece of paper in front of the cleaning lady. "Did you drop this prescription?"

"Not me, thank you. I don't have any prescriptions at all."

"Oh, dear," said the old woman. "Now someone has gone and lost a prescription for something that they may need to keep them alive, and here I've found it. What am I to do?" She tucked the prescription into her clothing somewhere. "I'll tell you this may be the thing that means life or death to some poor soul."

Slake knew something about life and death, even though he didn't know he knew it, and he had never thought that a piece of paper could be the answer.

"I have a brother," the old woman said chummily to the cleaning lady, "who has been sick for forty of his fifty years and you know what keeps him alive—a prescription. Goes right to the spot. Keeps him going."

The cleaning lady nodded, and started to rummage in her purse for something and Slake knew she was trying not to pay attention. He was getting to know things about her. The old woman also sensed this fact and turned to Slake, instead.

"I have a sister who has been sick with arthritis for seven years. If she lost a prescription it would mean a lot of pain. A lot of pain. Well, perhaps I can send it back to the doctor who gave it. See," and she fished into her clothing to retrieve the piece of paper. "Can you make out what it says? Is there a name on it?" She pushed one corner of the prescription at Slake, but wouldn't let go of her end. Connected thus with the old woman—connected by a piece of paper that held the life or death of some unknown person—Slake felt oddly in touch with the flow of the world. The paper was old, quite brittle and yellow and what was written on it was not legible to him. He shook his head.

"There," said the old woman, and back it went into the files of her body. "In fact, I'm the only well person in my family. I have an aunt who is now ninety-three, if you believe that. Ninety-three!" Slake knew no reason not to believe it. "I've taken care of her for twenty-five years. I was still not much more than a young woman when I started. I thought she was dying. Well, she's been kept alive all these years on a prescription, too. 'Millie, this; Millie that,' is the way it goes all day. Thirty years is a long time. . . ."

Slake now knew a lot about this old woman. Her name must be Millie. She had a fifty-year-old brother who'd been sick for forty years. She had a sister with arthritis, and despite this bad family history her own health was fine. She also had an old aunt whom she'd taken care of for twenty-five or thirty years, and she had now found a prescription, the responsibility of which weighed on her heavily. All these things Slake knew about a woman who had been unknown to him only a few minutes ago and who now, as the train came into sight, turned away without a farewell. Slake thought he would probably not see her again and he was not sorry. He was not glad, but he was not sorry. This old woman did not bring good feelings with her, but Slake felt something about her. What? He watched her square back until it disappeared into the sealed subway capsule and was swallowed by the tunnel.

The next time the rat returned could have been a dream of the last visit. As soon as Slake began to eat, smearing the ketchup on his saltines, the rat appeared, an emaciated phantom at the doorway. Slake's lifelong dislike of rats was blunted somewhat by this opportunity to study one so closely. What he knew about rats was all bad. Yet here was a rat which he could see for himself was not hostile—envious, perhaps, and greedy—but not hostile. It hunched at the entrance like a passerby looking into a restaurant window. And that thought, fleeting though it was, caused Slake, without really meaning to do so, to throw a small crumb on the floor of the room. The rat waited only long enough for the crumb to fall, and then he was down on the floor licking it from the rock.

Why should Slake's eyes tear? What could touch him about a dirty, infested rodent, eating a crumb on a rock floor? Slake coughed on his cracker and rubbed a fist in his eyes. The rat stayed where he was, putting his nose down again to the rock, searching. Slake took another bite of his cracker and regarded the rat who now looked directly at Slake. And again, without planning it, Slake threw another piece of cracker. The rat had the crumb in less time than it took to make its arc in the air.

And so Slake shared the rest of his breakfast with the rat. When the last bit was consumed by each, Slake rose suddenly from the table and the rat leaped up and out through the entrance as if pursued.

When had anyone or anything ever feared Slake? Never.

ON ANOTHER TRACK

The idea of sheepherding became so natural for Willis Joe that before long people began to *look* like sheep to him. Perhaps it was the hypnotizing effect of the track slipping under the train which, unlike jogging around Randall's Island, did not make all thoughts go out of his mind, but left them free to brood. But there was more than that. Willis Joe never forgot what his granny had told him, and when he drove an express train whizzing by the stations, people started to look like sheep to him because their souls were blurred by the speed of the train. After a while it just became a habit to think of them that way.

There were all kinds of sheep—old gummers and broken-mouthed sheep, wooled sheep and clippers, drop-bands . . . the lot. Sometimes he would survey a herd shoving its way into the cars and he would ask himself which was the lead sheep—the sheep which stopped, started, and turned the flock. What Willis Joe did not know, and would not know for quite a while, was that if, indeed, the people *were* sheep, he was not the herder that he thought he was, but *the lead sheep.*

When it happened, it was an important point in the life of Willis Joe Whinny, but it was also important in the life of Aremis Slake.

Slake had separated himself from the keeping of time and dates. Although the newspaper carried this news too, it had no importance to Slake in his world on the other side of the stones. Still he did know it was deep into winter because of people's wet boots, snow still clinging to them, and even in his warm jacket he felt the chill. And then one day it was ice.

"A genuine ice storm," a man said. "Nearly slipped and broke my neck right outside the Commodore."

"You could have sued them then," his companion reassured him.

Slake was in the middle of making change that morning when the lights went out on the platform. It was nearly total blackness, and at first it was quite impossible to see anything.

"What is it!"

"Why did . . . ?"

"What . . . ?"

Questions in the dark.

"Stand still," a voice called strongly. "Stand perfectly still. The light will come on again soon and if you move about you may fall or you may push someone off the platform, or be pushed."

Someone screamed at that.

"Just stand still."

Slake had known dark places, but he had never known one so black.

"It's probably just another of those power blackouts." The voice was right next to Slake and he knew it was the cleaning lady. "All the same I'm nervous. Here, take my hand," she said. "We'll keep each other from getting scared. Well, maybe you're not scared, but I am."

One of the few things in life that did not frighten Slake was the dark. He was used to groping around through his hazy world, and used now to living in a cave in a tunnel. The dark held a shield between him and the truth. He felt reasonably safe in it. He let the lady clutch his hand.

When had Slake last held the hand of anyone? He did not know. Not in his memory. Had he ever held Joseph's hand? He thought not.

"Evolution seems to have brought us back to this spot," someone laughed as he spoke. Slake knew the voice of the man with the turban. "Maybe thirty-five feet below ground is where we are now—burrowers in the earth. Blind. Perhaps evolution has reversed itself." The man laughed again. "*De*-volution," he said. "Ha, ha! *De*-volution!"

And the lights came on and revealed a tableau like a game that Slake used to see little kids playing on the playground—statues—everyone frozen in place; Slake, frozen with his hand in the hand of the cleaning lady.

Then, as if the switch were also thrown that

moved the bodies, motion began. The train lights appeared. Slake withdrew his hand and finished counting the change, and everyone moved toward the train.

The blackout had delayed Slake's sales and he waited on the platform for a few more trains. He was about to climb the stairs to go to his morning job in the restaurant when there was a scramble of feet and some shouting from above: "He's stolen my purse! Stop him!"

"Not me!" Slake screamed inside.

Down the stairs scrambled a boy of Slake's size, dodging under arms, around bodies.

"Stop him!"

Several people on the platform took this as a command, though most ignored it, and there was a pursuit down the length of the platform. The boy dropped the purse, and while his pursuers stopped to pick it up, he let himself over the edge, even as Slake had, and disappeared into the tunnel before the pack had reached him.

A transit policeman now appeared and jumped down onto the tracks and walked carefully into the tunnel.

"He'll never catch him," Slake told himself. The boy had a technique that suggested he'd done this before. But where must he run? To the next station? And would someone be waiting to pick him up there? Would he escape through some fire exit? Or would he hide, like Slake, in the tunnel's fastnesses? Were there other exiles here, then . . . other caves? Slake did not know.

That night Slake had two frightening dreams and he dreamed them again on other nights. In one dream he was drowsing in his cave when a boy hurtled through the porthole and found him there. They fought for the cave, and Slake woke up with a cry, not knowing who had won.

In the other dream, Slake returned home to his cave in the late afternoon to find the rat on the outside, waiting. Neither of them could find the hole to the cave. Had it been sealed up?

Slake awoke from such dreams with his heart beating loudly in his ears, and the bird scratching at his ribs. He felt no hunger for breakfast and gave it all to the rat. On such days darkness fell on Slake.

Sundays had a way of announcing themselves in the form of a change of rhythm. The station stayed quiet in the early morning hours when it was usually busiest. Slake would lie abed in supreme luxury in a way he had never done before in his life. He took his breakfast at leisure, sharing with the rat. He even felt some satisfaction in the fact that the rat's appearance had improved. On a Sunday too, there was not the accompanying fear of old that tomorrow meant school and another day of harassment by his classmates and teachers. His stomach did not churn and the bird within did not cry out. He devoted Sundays, usually, to the exploration of outlying districts, making odd-lot choices that did not fit into his scheme, especially. Just however he might wish to go. He might take it into his head to survey the tracks of the IND as they branched out into Queens to their outposts in Jamaica . . . the outer limits of his world. He could choose what he wished. This was freedom.

The station's usual early-morning quiet was startled, one Sunday, with singing and calling—a mélange of bright raucous noise. Slake put on his thready sneakers and poked his head out of his cave. Water was dripping somewhere . . . drip, drip, forming a puddle in the track bed near Slake's home. He slid into the tunnel and moved over to the platform. Keeping his body well below the platform level, he raised his head high enough to see what was going on. His view through his patchwork glasses from this angle of elevation gave him a sort of mosaic or kaleido-scopic image. Shifting abstractions. He adjusted his lenses until the source of the noise came into view. It was a group of young men, women, and children, dressed in jeans and warm caps and scarves. They were all carrying signs. The sing-ing and the hearty talk continued. They had a longer wait than usual because the train schedule was different on Sundays, so as they amused themselves Slake had ample time to look them over. A boy tossed his cap in the air and it landed not far from Slake. He ran laughing down the platform after it, waving his sign, which read:

SAVE THE EAST SIDE

When the train came in, there was a crush for the doors. The lights from the train filled the puddle at Slake's feet with moons, as Slake crouched now, well beneath the platform and out of the way of the train. The track bed became a lighted night sky.

Now the sign carriers were inside and away. Save the East Side from what, Slake thought. But even so, it was not the East Side so much that attracted him as the enormous enthusiasm of the people who held the signs. Till now Slake had not known he lacked a cause. There was nothing that Slake knew of that he wanted to save from anyone or for anyone the way these people seemed to want to save the East Side.

Slake returned to his cave, fixed his breakfast and shared it with the rat, who knew no Sunday. Then he went to his collection of art supplies and selected several cans of spray paint and Magic Markers. These were so plentiful in subway trash cans and on the tracks of the tunnels near the train yards that he now had a full palette of colors, even though the cans were nearly empty. He had used some to decorate his mobiles and other constructions, and he had painted his dining table a swirling mixture of blue and white. Now he took a can, shook it, and aiming at one of his newspaper-covered walls, sprayed in red paint:

SAVE

Yes, save. But save what? Slake's imagination did not take him far afield. He picked up another can and in electric blue sprayed:

AREMIS SLAKE

Slake sat down and regarded his work. He got some sort of feeling from it. Good . . . but beyond that he could not identify it. He had enjoyed the act of writing it.

Now Slake took up some other cans and began to idly spray the walls. He made some squares of color. Perhaps they were houses. He put roofs on them. He made a brown tree. And now he sprayed a large area above the houses for a sky. It was green.

Some might quarrel with Slake and say that skies are not green . . . or only when the light and clouds are just so. Seldom perhaps, but now for Slake, always. For the rest of his days underground this was the sky. Slake had not spent a lot of his life before this looking at the sky. He had spent most of it looking at his feet to make sure he did not step off into thin air, or looking over his shoulder to be sure he was not being pursued. Now, however, Slake spent considerable time looking at the sky, and it was green.

ON ANOTHER TRACK

At the terminal Willis Joe threw twenty-five cents into a football pool that the men were running. He bought a Coca-Cola from the vending machine. He looked briefly at the headlines of a paper that was spread out on the bench. He was killing time. Why?

As the winter dreared its way along and March came on, Willis Joe had been feeling inexplicably depressed. He was tired of herding baa-baas in winter and he was stuck with it. The thousands of sheep now began to fill him with distaste. He began to dislike going to work in the mornings, but more than that, he began to put off going home to his wife and children. The truth is that even they had begun to look like the creatures of the subway—like sheep. He had begun to quarrel with his wife frequently, and to yell at Wilma and Joe. He began to drive the train angrily, moving the brake handle sharply from the switching position, increasing his speed and taking downhill grades faster than he should—driving, driving.

Now, when he could no longer dawdle around the terminal and still get home for dinner, he took the subway, himself a passenger, deadheaded back to Thirty-sixth Avenue, and walked the long blocks to his house.

Willis Joe Whinny was on the edge . . . the very edge.

What are the chances of any two particular objects in space intercepting each other?

12 The accident must have happened when Slake was out for the afternoon on an extended tour of Brooklyn, taking the IND back up the West Side, shuttling over and arriving at Grand Central on the lower level of tracks. As soon as he arrived at the station he sensed something was wrong. This level was not usually so crowded at this time of day. The people were noisy and talking together instead of quietly or restlessly waiting for trains. The stairway was jammed.

Slake snaked up a staircase, holding close to the yellow and blue handrail. But when he tried to make his way to the downtown platform and his home, he found his path barred by policemen who were putting up barricades. *What was wrong?* The bird in Slake cried those words because whatever it was—fire, crash, loss of power—Slake was cut off from his home, and this knowledge made little of whatever tragedy may have struck the tunnel. The only person in full focus in Slake's life was Slake; other people could only be blurs, hurrying by. They were forces, not people. And so the bird cried, but it cried for Slake.

A voice was giving directions on the loudspeaker. "The downtown tracks of the IRT are temporarily out of service due to an accident in the tunnel. Please find alternate routes to your destinations."

"The concrete in that tunnel has been cracking up for years," a transit policeman said, as he moved past Slake.

A guard replied, "Yep, there's some holes in there big enough to drive a train through."

Holes! They'd found his cave! The bird was pecking at Slake's ribs so that he thought he'd cry out himself.

"But I've always taken the same train. Now how am I going to get home from here?" A lady complained. Slake could have told her. He had become a leading expert in the matter of getting there from here. It was his major subject of organized knowledge. But he did not volunteer, and his talent was not used by the scores of people that day, or any day, who, their usual routes blocked, sought escape by some other underground passage. Slake could have told them all how to go home, but he could not tell himself. Now he could see the workmen going down the stairs to the track bed. What were they going to do?

The loudspeaker again: "The downtown tracks are temporarily blocked by falling concrete. Please find alternate routes to your destinations. It is expected that the track will be closed for several hours."

People continued to arrive for the downtown train, and the guards were kept busy redirecting them. Slake redirected himself back to the shuttle. He didn't care where he went. He was only passing time until he could go home.

"Go home!" Those words had come to mean something to Slake as they had never done before. A place of his own. My place, Slake now thought. Going to my place. And as surely as any explorer who had first set foot anywhere—the Arctic, the moon—Slake was certainly at least one of the few and only settlers on this piece of a dark continent in the subway and had, if he wished, every right to call it his. Slake's home, Slake's cave, Slake's space between—Slake's limbo.

When Slake returned in the evening the station was still roped off, and he went to the uptown platform to see what he could see from there. There was a train in the station on the downtown side. Some windows were broken in the front car. The top of the car looked dented. It looked like a bruised fighter. Crews of workmen were in the tunnel; he could see that. Were they working near his cave? There was no chance to get past them. Not a chance in the world.

Slake returned to ride the subway for the night, along with the little old ladies in long coats who slept the night in the cars, carrying all their worldly goods in a shopping bag. How much more fortunate than they was Slake with a room of his own. But anxiety about his home followed Slake up and down the East and West sides, and out to Brooklyn and back. He did not stay on one train for fear of being found by the transit police who rode the trains at night. So he took short naps rather than sleeps, rising occasionally to switch trains. But his inner clock worked and morning found him at his regular task of picking up and folding papers.

"Well, here's my paper!" the cleaning lady said cheerily to Slake as he approached. "And how are you this morning?" She was used to no answers from Slake. But when she looked at him as she handed him the change, she said, "Well, you don't look chipper, I'll say that. You're not sick, are you?" Slake shook his head. "You look pale. You kids don't get enough rest. I know. I have a son, you know." Slake knew. The lady went on, "You take my advice and take it a little slower. Don't be in such a hurry. Live gentle. Live gentle and get to bed early. Okay?" Slake nodded and she took her paper.

When Slake took up his broom at the luncheonette, the vigor and enthusiasm that he had been able to bring to sweeping was not with him. If something stubbornly stuck to the floor, Slake did not feel motivated to dislodge it. He swept not like the master of the broom but like an extension of the broom handle.

When he sat down for his lunch, the waitress said, "Well, you look bushed!" and she gave him a glass of orange juice to start on. "Take that. It's quick energy I heard a doctor say on TV." It felt good in Slake's throat. He'd had no breakfast that morning and his mouth and throat were dry and hot.

The waitress and the manager conversed and included Slake in the circle of their talk.

"Hear about the accident last night down on the downtown tracks?" Slake nodded. "What's amazing is that it didn't happen before. They've been patching it and patching it for years. Linemen come in here and talk to me. I know. Blasting for big buildings all around here doesn't help it. Lucky it wasn't worse. This time they can call it an accident, but next time people will be calling it negligence, you know. Now they'll just *have* to fix that tunnel."

Slake choked, "They're going to fix it?"

"Bet your life they're going to fix it."

"When?"

"When! When the city can gather up all the red tape it takes to get a crew down here with some reinforced concrete."

"How soon?"

"Dunno. There's something in the paper about it, but I haven't read it all."

The waitress now looked closely at Slake. She

had never seen him so interested in anything before.

"Why?" she asked Slake, as she served him his lunch. "What do you care when?"

Why did she ask! Slake dropped his head as the waitress placed a small bag of food beside his plate. He ate very little, pushed the plate away, grabbed the bag and left.

"Take care," the waitress called after him.

13 Slake took care. He went down the stairs to the downtown track without any hindrances. The police had left; the barricades were piled to one side. The normal flow of traffic had resumed. There was a train in the station now and Slake waited for it to pull out. Then he crept over the edge of the platform and down the track to his hole in the wall. Once inside the cave he lit one of his lanterns and sat down to try and find the story in the newspaper. The first page told of an air crash, two killings downtown, a war someplace Slake had never heard of, and a polar bear dying in the zoo. But at the bottom of the page a two-column story announced the bad news:

16 Injured in IRT
By Falling Concrete

The story went on to say that a train just leaving the downtown platform of the IRT at Grand Central had been struck by concrete falling from the walls of the old tunnel. The first car had been damaged and several people, including the motorman, had been hurt by broken glass and the sudden impact. There had been no fatalities. Spokesmen for the Metropolitan Transit Authority said that all the loose concrete had been removed and there was no immediate danger. As soon as trains could be re-routed, the tunnel would be closed, all surfaces carefully examined for cracks, and permanent repairs begun. The tunnel had been slated for renovation for a long time but the inconvenience to the public made postponement necessary. (Now the story was continued on page sixteen and Slake turned the pages until he found it.) Here was a photograph of the damaged train just as Slake had seen it last night. It gave him an odd feeling to have seen this very thing before it appeared in the newspaper—like a dream or a prophecy.

The rest of the story named the injured who had been hospitalized and gave a firsthand account by the motorman, Mr. Carmine Alvirez. Mr. Alvirez said this was bound to happen sooner or later and it was just fate that it happened to him. He didn't blame anyone. He just thanked God that it wasn't a really terrible tragedy where someone got killed.

The story concluded with the information that suggestions for alternate travel would be given in a few days and work would be undertaken at that time.

Slake read his death sentence. His knowledge of construction was limited mostly to its opposite—demolition—great yellow cranes swinging large iron balls doing battle with crippled old bricks. Not a fair fight. Even with this little experience Slake knew what was in store for him. If he had been trained as a subway architect and engineer he could not have been surer. The machines and men would soon start to creep down the track, foot by foot, until they reached Slake's hole, and like the other cracks, breaks, holes, and faults in this old tunnel, the entrance to Slake's home would be covered over.

The bird in Slake screamed!

At first Slake stayed in his cave out of anxiety and depression which grew to pure misery. He sat hunched against the back wall of the Commodore Hotel, soon to have an unused room once again. Or would it soon possess a tomb?

By the end of the second day, Slake had not eaten for more than thirty hours. His fatigue from the long night's journey on the train combined with lack of nourishment made him feel cold and weak. By midnight, his illness which had up to then been fear, was complicated by chills and fever. He felt cold and wrapped himself in layers and layers of newspapers. Then he felt hot and tore them off. He was empty but not hungry. He was terribly thirsty but he would not take the cans out for water. He would not leave his home. They might seal it while he was gone.

He fell into light, short sleeps in which there was no rest. He was in a vacant lot. Where? He was on his knees and he was digging a hole in the ground with his bare hands, prying the earth loose and kicking it. In the hole, Slake buried a sweater, a sweater with triangles of blue and gray.

Slake was in a chair that spun around. It was spun by the man with the turban. Round and round Slake spun. He wished to get off but the man would not let him. The waitress in the luncheonette said, "Let him off. Let him off." She offered him a drink of orange juice. Slake put out his hand for the juice but he could not reach it.

Slake was on the street. Was that his old block? The wind was blowing. It blew through Slake's shirt and he was cold. The sun came out and he tore off the shirt.

In the slough of Slake's dreams, snakes and crocodiles snapped and slashed, gnashed and thrashed. Dank and clammy, then steamy and hot, the swamp rose and fell over him, or he into and out of it, through the days and nights of his infection.

The bird in Slake cried piteously those days.

Slake did not know when he was awake or asleep. Sometimes he thought he was asleep and he was awake, and sometimes he thought he was awake and he was asleep. He did not know how many days went by. He did not know that the rat came daily. The first day it ate well on the contents of the paper bag Slake had carried home and dropped on the floor. After that, the rat came and waited and left . . . every day.

And then, during one of his waking periods, Slake heard unfamiliar sounds in the tunnel—sounds of hammering. In the days that had just passed, the cause of the illness that had brought Slake down had been forgotten by him. But now, the sounds in the tunnel made Slake's mind very clear. *They were coming!* The crowbars, the wreckers, the cement mixers were coming.

Slake pulled himself up from the paper bed in which he had lain all these days. He groped for the piece of cardboard that he knew was near the entrance. Then, slowly, deliberately, Slake took a felt pen and wrote four large letters in red on the board.

Leaning out of his porthole he could make out the shape of what he believed to be a repair vehicle standing in the station, its white eyeballs alight. He regarded the tracks and third rail, a crocodile and snakes lurking outside his cave. And now Slake joined them, dragging himself over the edge of his den and into the tunnel.

ON ANOTHER TRACK

Willis Joe Whinny had stopped his train at the downtown platform of Grand Central Station. This would be the last run on this route before repairs began. The white light had signaled that the doors were all closed and he was just about to start up when the door of his compartment swung open. That latch had been a nuisance all day and this time he swore he'd fix it to stay fixed. He removed the brake handle and using it for a hammer gave the latch a few good whacks. When he tried the door it was better but still not secure so he gave it a few more light taps with the brake. Right. He could now get back to the everlasting job of moving these baa-baas to market. He checked the air and pipe pressure readings, and moved the brake into the switching position, and the train began to move forward. He wanted to make up for lost time now. And then he saw it—a stray on the road-bed ahead. Well, you always lose a few. . . . But then he saw the sign. It said

STOP

and in that tearing second Willis Joe Whinny knew that *he* was the lead sheep and he stopped the train.

14 Willis Joe was out on the track in the next ten seconds picking up the collapsed and fallen Slake, the cardboard sign tumbled on the tracks beside him. Willis Joe stood on the tracks and held him as he had once held his new son and daughter and stared at Slake who lay ashen in his arms. And Willis Joe Whinny started to quake.

People had now run to the front of the car to see what had happened and with their help Willis Joe laid Slake on the floor of the car while he climbed back up. Then he lifted Slake and carried him in his arms the whole length of the ten-car train. A transit policeman had boarded the train at the last car and Willis Joe surrendered his burden.

"We'll need a complete report on this," the policeman said. "You check in with us when you finish your run."

Now Willis Joe walked back through the train to his car looking into the faces of the people who had watched his progress through the train. And he could see now that they were not blurred at all, and that each one of them was a single person like him, and he thought that he could clearly see that every one of them had a soul.

Now he drove his train attentively as if it were a mission and he, a motorman, had a calling. Back there were hundreds of people who looked to him to take them safely from their homes to their work and back again, to trundle their children safely through the city caverns. And something else touched Willis Joe with importance. He knew that in another few hours he could go home to his wife and children.

It was in the ambulance that Slake opened his eyes. There was a mask clamped over his nose and mouth. There were voices but they were only hums and not important to him. He did not know or care where he was. He felt no panic. There was a window at his side and through it, when he opened his eyes, he could see the buildings outlined against the sky. The sky was blue not green, and this seemed important to him. Slake slipped back into something like sleep.

Willis Joe made his report and spoke with the transit cop.

"They goin' to charge him?" Willis Joe asked.

The officer watched Willis Joe closely as he spoke. "Well, I don't think so," he said, and he was trying to see into Willis Joe's head. "This kid has pneumonia or something. He can hardly breathe. He's in shock. It looks to me like he was real sick and confused and just ran out on the track."

"That's how it looked to me," said Willis Joe.

After Willis Joe made his report he went to

Bellevue Hospital to find out if he could see Slake. He could not. The boy was in an oxygen tent, they said, and they still did not know his name. But Willis Joe went out and bought a card and brought it back to the hospital and left it at the desk. It was addressed to "The Boy In The Subway" and it reached Slake some days later when he was feeling better. It was a big card with a bouquet of flowers pressed out so that you could feel the flowers. Inside there were very fancy letters which read, "Thinking of you," and it was signed "Willis Joe Whinny" in Willis Joe's own handwriting.

Slake, when he received this first piece of mail in his whole life, was more astounded at having received it at all than by the fact that he did not know who Willis Joe Whinny was. The world was full of people who he did not know and that wasn't important to him. What was important was the odd fact that someone was thinking of Slake.

15 The comfort of the days in the hospital—the real mattress, the hot meals served in bed, the incredible warmth—balanced to a large degree the discomfort in Slake's head and chest, the weakness, and the lack of freedom of action.

In those days Slake often thought of his home in the subway and he felt a kind of pain when he visualized the gay lantern-lit carnival of his mobiles casting their shadows in his private room, as the trains and life whizzed by. But as the days passed, he began to feel like those people in his neighborhood who used to say their apartments had burned or their landlords had turned them out and kept their things and they had "lost everything." That they had "everything" to lose had always colored Slake's proper sympathy. Now he too had sustained a loss—his home, his worldly goods. He, Slake!

As he lay abed before sleeping, he imagined darkly that they were now cementing the porthole to his cave, sealing it forever as if it were an Egyptian tomb such as he knew from school books—sealing the tomb of Aremis Slake with all his possessions and provisions so that his soul might eat. But was the soul of Aremis Slake in the tomb? Slake thought not. He had escaped the tomb. Life everlasting, thought Slake that night as he fell asleep above ground.

The bird in Slake, which had been breathing quietly, was somewhat disturbed by the visit of a social worker who, young and anxious, inquired of Slake's family, Slake's home. None, none. Slake shook his head vaguely. But he must live someplace—with a friend? Slake shook his head variously, only confusing the young woman wishing to help.

"Don't you worry. We'll look after you. You'll stay here until you are well, and then we'll see what sort of juvenile facility you can fit into until we can locate your people. You just rest and get well now. I'll come back. Is there something you'd like?"

"My clothes," said Slake. "My glasses."

The social worker spoke to the floor supervisor and, in the days that followed, Slake's clothes, which seemed to have disappeared, were replaced by some clean clothes that fitted quite well, and he was given an eye examination and some glasses. Also returned to Slake was a sealed brown envelope which contained his wallet, and keys, and the change that had been in his pockets.

"You might want to buy something from the carts," said the floor supervisor.

But Slake did not like the thought of a "juvenile facility." He got anxious about the idea. Nevertheless, everything was so effortless and agreeable right now that he almost wished the illness might last a bit longer. Almost . . . but Slake had seen the sky blue, and for the first time since that day in November when he had entered the subway at Columbus Circle, he felt a strong desire to see it blue again . . . to feel it, to be in it.

Slake thought on it, and finally made some plans. The bird quieted. In fact it became so quiet that in the middle of one night Slake dreamed the bird had died, and he did not know if it would be more dreadful to have inside him a live or a dead bird. He slept in fits, but toward morning the bird began to flutter again among Slake's ribs as he slept. With a great deal of tossing and straining, Slake retched and the bird flew free. Slake felt it go. He awoke suddenly, aware, alert, but not in time to see the bird leave. Had it flown out into the corridors, now trapped not in Slake's stomach but in the hospital? How would it be treated when found? Slake's throat was dry and hurt, but his chest and stomach were free of its flutter.

Who remembers the first day he saw daylight? Some perhaps, but in particular, one, Aremis Slake. Slake was now about to be born.

When the day came that Slake felt well enough and strong enough, he liberated himself from the hospital, not waiting for the pleasant social worker to find him a "facility." He stood

115

outside the building taking gulps of air. It tasted of spring, but yet there was an aftertaste of winter. Slake's first impression of himself was that he had grown taller. There was nothing to measure it against. He could not even say he had outgrown his clothes because these were not his old clothes. Yet, yes, he was certainly taller. Or perhaps it was the angle from which he saw things—not peering at the sidewalk, but straight out and across and even up? Because it was amazing what the new glasses did to the world. Distances that had never existed before were drawn in clearly. And, as he raised his eyes to the buildings and the blue sky, he saw a bird sitting on the ledge of a building. And what building? The hospital! And what bird? His bird? There *was* that possibility. Had it escaped then? It stayed only a moment and took wing. It had been with him too long and they were free of each other.

You see real good, Slake told himself. To run; to sweep; to see! What else!

It might be said of Slake that he had spent all of his life on the underside of the stones. For the first time now he became sharply aware that he was walking *on* not under. And yet he did not want to stay on these streets. Instinct turned him toward the nearest subway entrance, but as he reached it and started down, he stopped, turned, and looked at the sky again. How fortunate the bird that had fled from Slake, released to the sky! Slake brought his eyes down a bit. If not the sky for *him*, might he look to the reality of the roofs? Slake was not innocent of roofs. He knew they had abandoned water tanks, old elevator housings, untended pigeon coops. From one of these he could see the sky every day—blue or even gray if must be.

But then what of the cleaning lady, the man with the turban, the waitress, his job, the rat? The rat was now walled out, like Slake himself. He knew that. The others . . . he would see them sometime soon, perhaps, but not now. Right now Slake had something he had to do.

He turned and started up the stairs and out of the subway. Slake did not know exactly where he was going, but the general direction was up.

ABOUT THE AUTHOR

Felice Holman was born in New York City and raised in its suburbs. She is the author of many distinguished books for young people—among them *The Escape of the Giant Hogstalk, I Hear You Smiling and other poems, The Future of Hooper Toote,* and *The Cricket Winter.* She now lives in Connecticut.